In
Hugger-Mugger

*Dark Secrets and Forbidden Love
in Renaissance England*

JOYCE GATTA

In Memory of

Janet D. McLean

(1937-2020)

© Joyce Gatta 2020

ISBN: 978-1-09832-579-4

eBook ISBN: 978-1-09832-580-0

All rights reserved. This book or any portion thereof may not be reproduced or used in any manner whatsoever without the express written permission of the publisher except for the use of brief quotations in a book review.

Renaissance—a period of revived intellectual or artistic achievement or enthusiasm

The Renaissance (1300s–1600s) was a period of intense intellectual curiosity and a time in which British subjects tested the power of the church and the monarchy in governing people's behavior.

Literary academies, which promoted the exchange of knowledge and ideas, sprung up in plain view, while secret societies, perhaps working to overthrow the Church of England, or else dabbling in mystical and scientific theories, operated underground.

Women, in particular, became more educated and began to work in fields that had previously been acceptable to men only. A few began to write and publish, a few began to practice medicine, and a few secretly defied the Church and Crown to marry whomever they chose.

Contents

Preface xi

BOOK ONE
Mary Sidney, Countess of Pembroke 1
Chapter One 3
Chapter Two 6
Chapter Three 13
Chapter Four 21
Chapter Five 25
Chapter Six 30
Chapter Seven 36
Chapter Eight 42

BOOK TWO
Sarah Burton and Robert Dudley 49
Chapter One 51
Chapter Two 53
Chapter Three 58
Chapter Four 66
Chapter Five 71
Chapter Six 84
Chapter Seven 89
Chapter Eight 92
Chapter Nine 99
Chapter Ten 103
Chapter Eleven 109
Chapter Twelve 114
Chapter Thirteen 119
Chapter Fourteen 123

Chapter Fifteen...129

Chapter Sixteen...133

Chapter Seventeen..137

Chapter Eighteen...143

Chapter Nineteen...149

Chapter Twenty...151

Chapter Twenty-one..154

Chapter Twenty-two..159

Chapter Twenty-three...165

Chapter Twenty-four...170

BOOK THREE
Mary Sidney and her son William Herbert................179

Chapter One..181

Chapter Two...186

Chapter Three...190

Chapter Four...194

Chapter Five...197

Chapter Six...201

Chapter Seven..203

BOOK FOUR
Sarah Burton and Mary Sidney....................................207

Chapter One..209

Chapter Two...215

Chapter Three...218

Chapter Four...222

Chapter Five...227

Epilogue..234

Author's Note...237

Bibliography...241

About the author..243

Preface

On a hot, steamy morning in late August of 1621, while many of London's wealthy inhabitants had left the city to escape the sultry weather and the accompanying diseases it bred, a magnificent horse-drawn carriage pulled up in front of a building in the Barbican area of the city, near the River Thames. The Barbican was known for being very Puritan; it had no theatres, but because of its cheap rents, it did draw in theatrical types. The location had once been the home of William Shakespeare as well as Ben Jonson. but they had long ago moved on to better lodgings. It was now the home of shops like tanners, tallow melters, charcoal sellers and printers.

Inside the coach sat two passengers who had been compelled to go there in spite of the sweltering heat. The space within the carriage was entirely enclosed so that not even a slight breeze from the nearby river could find an opening to give them relief. The crest on the door of the gilded, ornate vehicle had been deliberately covered over, providing no hint as to the identity of its occupants—a countess and her doctor.

The noblewoman was wrapped in fine dark linens and wore a black lacy veil over her face, giving her a stately but somber look. Behind the veil was the countenance of an elderly yet still handsome lady. She was in very good health for a woman of fifty-nine years of age. Her long oval face was framed by tiny puffs of curls, once bright red but now decidedly gray, each one coiled like springs in a clock. Her bright eyes darted to and fro as if on alert for any sign of trouble. Across from her sat a dark-haired, bearded doctor, who was also her lover. Handsome in face and figure, with large, somewhat droopy eyes, his overall appearance made him look approachable and trustworthy. Although he was also clothed in black, his soft smile and relaxed posture was in stark contrast to that of his companion.

The door of the vehicle was opened by a footman, and the noble-woman nodded to her companion. He, in turn, picked up a large purse with one hand and a heavy package with the other and, handing them to the footman to hold, climbed out. The door of the carriage closed, and the lady assumed her rigid posture, unconsciously clutching and then smoothing the folds of her garments as she waited for him to return.

The doctor, burdened down by his bundles, walked slowly up to the storefront. He passed under a sign that read *The Half-Eagle and Key*. Once inside, he asked to speak to the owners in private and was ushered into the offices of Messieurs Jaggard and Blount. There, he explained his errand and laid down his offerings— the "fair" copies of five unlicensed plays to be published and a large sum of money to pay for their labor. Although he was pressed to give his name, he refused, saying simply, "There will be many more plays and much more money to follow." He promised to be back in a few months and assured the printers that the Lord Chamberlain would not try to stop their publication, even though it was illegal to publish works that were unlicensed. The printers protested strenuously to such conditions.

"Sir, we cannot do this. We are a reputable firm, and it is against the law to print works without a license."

"And I assure you that there will be no reprisal from the Lord Chamberlain. He will not object to the printing of these particular plays. I give you my word as a gentleman."

IN HUGGER-MUGGER

The owners looked at the well-dressed individual standing before them and then at the bulging purse lying on their desk. They moved to a corner and quietly conferred with each other. Finally they turned to face their visitor and agreed, reluctantly, to begin the printing forthwith.

The man left, climbed back into the carriage, and smiled at his companion, Lady Mary Sidney. She exhaled and leaned forward to grasp the hands of her doctor and lover, Matthew Lister.

"Everything is going exactly as planned," she whispered, even though there was no one nearby who could possibly hear. "My son will not be able to stop the printing. I have outwitted him at last. Nothing can prevent all my plays from being published now."

Relishing what they had just done, the two of them settled back for the short ride to the safety of their home on Aldgate Street and protection from the pox that was now running rampant throughout London.

One month later, the countess was dead and the printing had stopped.

BOOK ONE
Mary Sidney, Countess of Pembroke

Chapter One

Fall 1592
London
Rumblings in the Mermaid Tavern

It was the first Friday of the month, the time when the members of the so-called "Fraternity of Sireniacal Gentlemen" met to gossip, like old crones yapping on about a prigman who stole clothes that were drying in the fields or about a dell seen on the road begging for food. Only these rumormongers were writers and actors who knew that they could bring down their rival's reputation if their tales were told with a straight face and enough particulars to be convincing. An actor from the Rose Theater Company leaned over his flagon of ale, trying to hear what was being said just across the scared and battered oak table, littered with food scraps, and empty beer mugs.

"What's that you say, Tom?"

His fellow Thespian turned around and shouted above the din, "I said yet another play has been printed with Will Shakespeare's name on the frontispiece. That makes yet another that he claims he augments or edits and then prints like they're his own. I say it's strange that an actor, and not a very good one at that, can write volumes of verse as if by magic."

"Agreed!", said the first speaker. "I've been in his company now and again and he never talks of writing plays. Seems to me like he's trying to pirate other people's works. I don't go in for that dirty business. It ain't right to steal someone else's labor."

"Robert Greene called him an upstart crow who can't even spell his own name the same way twice. Sounds about right to me. Who would believe, "continued Tom, "that such an actor could write about the history of England, battles of war, and life at court like he was actually there. Will never fought in a battle in his life or cozied up to royalty. And I've never seen him with a book in his hand. Edward, if Will Shakespeare is a playwright, then I am a king."

"Well, your majesty," said Edward dryly, "perhaps he writes 'em between curtain calls."

"Ha! Sure doesn't sound like our Will," Tom snorted. "He is usually around a lady when he isn't on stage."

A third fellow who has been gnawing on a chicken bone, shot his head up, spit a mouthful of gristle on the floor and cried out, "You know, that reminds me of something Greene said just before he died last month. He wrote a letter to his friends about Will. As I remember, he was none too keen that Will's plays were more popular than his own, maybe he was just jealous, but he said to look for a woman behind Shakespeare. None of us knew what to make of it."

"A woman? George, are you sure?" said Edward. That's an odd thing to say. Greene can't mean one of Shakespeare's strumpets is writing verse."

"Ha! You know about Will's womanizing, then. Hard to imagine a strumpet writing poesy," replied George. "But Greene was always clever and wily and he was not known to say foolish things. And —

listen to this — he said he found that someone had changed at least one of the Pembroke Players' scripts. He was certain of it."

Edward scratched his beard and called for another flagon of ale. "Now who would have the gall to change a script? Women ain't around scripts. Damn, most women can hardly read, never mind write."

"Woman or no woman, it sure isn't Will Shakespeare writing those plays, " Tom declared.

"If Greene was so sure it's a woman, he must have known know who it was. Why didn't he give out her name? Answer me that, " asked Edward.

George bent his head toward the other two men and winked before confiding, "I think this woman is high-placed, you know, a lady of noble birth and a good education. He couldn't say who it is because she might be a kin of the queen. That would have put him in hot water, indeed." He picked up a knife from his plate and made as if to slice his throat.

"Bad business, for sure. Now that Greene is dead, we may never know who he suspected was changing the scripts."

"No, but be on the lookout if you are ever with the Pembroke Players troupe."

Chapter Two

November 1600
Wilton House, Wiltshire, England
Mother and Daughter Secrets

"Marry him. That is the short and long of it."

There. It was said. Lady Mary Sidney Herbert, the Countess of Pembroke, had uttered the very words she knew her daughter, Lady Anne Herbert, loathed to hear. Queen Elizabeth had given permission for a nobleman, an elderly widower, to wed Lady Anne Herbert, who was just seventeen, and that was that.

Mother and daughter had secluded themselves by a desk in a far corner of the massive library at Wilton House, whispering so that their words did not echo across the room and into the hall where straining ears were certain to be found. The manor sat on an estate of forty-five thousand acres in the Wiltshire countryside with a tributary of the Avon River flowing by it. The property, although by far not the grandest residence among the English nobility, was particularly acclaimed for its grotto and water features. The house itself was an elegantly designed rectangular building built around a central courtyard, all in all an edifice fit to entertain a queen and it was her Royal Highness whose assent had to be secured in all marriages involving members of the nobility.

"Mother, I implore you. Do not ask me to do this."

"Dear Anne, I have no power to undo Elizabeth's charge. When the Crown decides on such matters, even I, her former lady-in-waiting, must obey. Such is the breath of a queen."

Mary Sidney Herbert understood only too well how the monarchy functioned. She was a cousin of Queen Elizabeth, six times removed, and even bore many similar facial features: curly red hair, oval face, sharp eyes, aquiline nose, and full mouth. She as well as her mother, had attended the queen and spent much time watching how Elizabeth used her power to keep tight control over her empire. Mary's own husband, now sixty-six and an invalid, had been chosen for her by Elizabeth when Mary was only fifteen and he forty-three. Henry Herbert, Earl of Pembroke, twice widowed and childless, had a hot temper and Mary learned early in their marriage that it was best to keep out of his presence as much as possible. She became involved in her own pursuits. Henry had allowed her time to experiment with various herbs and chemicals and to entertain literary figures as she wished. But most especially, he had allowed her time to write. She began with a play that dwelt on war and revenge, murder and genocide. *Titus Andronicus* mirrored her mood on the futility of war for she had suffered the loss of her own dear brother in a battle that proved nothing and was lost to history. Writing the play was an outlet for her anger over men's desire to fight, which in turn, made those men suffer the loss of loved ones and then to revenge those losses by more killing.

Her husband also funded the Pembroke's Men, a troupe of actors who came there to perform plays in which Mary often participated. And he allowed her to regularly host a group of writers to discuss, dissect, and perfect each other's works. Their marriage was not an outgrowth of love but one she could bear. In many ways she was lucky to have such freedom, but she knew it to be highly unlikely that Anne would have similar liberties after her marriage to an elderly lord.

Now she smiled weakly at Anne who was sitting slumped over, eyes red from crying. The handkerchief in her daughter's hand was twisted around her fingers so tightly that the fabric was becoming undone, as was Anne's contented life, which, up to now, was woven in poetry and literature, history and science, dances and masques. Mary remembered how she herself had felt as a young noble lady, when Henry, newly widowed, had picked her for his new wife. She had accepted her fate as the trade-off for enjoying all the privileges of title and wealth. Anne had inherited her mother's beauty, intelligence, and spirit, but Mary had not anticipated that Anne would be so obstinate regarding her duty to marry a nobleman who had influence with the Crown. Among the harvest of young noble ladies in England in 1600, Anne Herbert was the pick of the crop. Everything a suitor could wish for, she had in surplus quantities: looks, wit, temper, and an impeccable lineage, along with an impressive dowry. No wonder that she had attracted the attention of many young swains as well as a few haughty and boring old goats. The sacrifice her daughter was expected to make would change the course of her young life, and she would have nothing to say about it. As far as Queen Elizabeth was concerned, love and marriage were two unrelated words.

"The Queen will expect you to accede to her wishes, and then you must obey, just as she asked for a play in which Falstaff falls in love, although the ending may not be what she expected. Unrequited love! In comedies, all for the better."

"Please, Mama. Do not speak about unrequited love. I am of marrying age, and if the Queen wants me to marry a man three times my age, as you had to do, I will kill myself rather than submit!" She reached for a letter opener that lay on her mother's desk and pushed the sharp end toward her chest, her eyes begging for her mother to find a way out of this dilemma..

Mary's smile faded quickly, and the library in which they were sitting, sixty feet in length, seemed to contract like a squeezed accordion. The air around the countess suddenly became heavy, and Mary shakily put down her swan quill pen and straighten the sheets of vellum stacked in front of her. Her eyes filled with tears at the thought of her only surviving daughter dying by her own hand.

"Tut, daughter. Those are but wild and whirling words. I will speak to the queen about your marriage prospects. Perhaps if I bring up young Robert Dudley's name again, the queen will reconsider."

She knew this to be unlikely since Elizabeth had already rejected him as a possible husband for Anne. The young Robert Dudley was Anne's third cousin, known to her since childhood and pleasing in figure and intellect. Elizabeth herself had been wooed by Robert Dudley's elder *cousin, a lord by the same name and an uncle to Mary Sidney.* The two men, cousins with powerful connections to the throne, were handsome, dashing noblemen, experienced in hunting and dancing and all the pleasures that the Court offered, but Elizabeth had dismissed Mary's uncle as her own husband, even though she loved him. It was improbable that she would be swayed by Lady Anne's desire to marry the younger cousin. After all, marriages among nobility had to strengthen the power of the monarchy; young Robert and Lady Anne's union would do no such thing. Anne was too big a prize to be married off to the second son of her distant cousin. Mary knew by suggesting young Robert Dudley as a possible husband for Anne, she was just appeasing her deeply depressed daughter.

"I pray that Robert is found to be acceptable, but the queen has rejected his cousin, your uncle, for her own husband whom everyone knows she adored. While he lived, Elizabeth and Sir Robert were often seen laughing and dancing together and there were even rumors of them bedding together."

"Hush, Anne. Such talk can get you beheaded."

"I want to be like the women in your plays where daughters outsmart their fathers or slaves their masters or subjects their kings and get to marry the ones they love. All the men I am coupled with are arrogant and callous ancients. I will never submit to such an arrangement. I plan to marry whomever I choose and fie on the queen!" Anne shouted, loud enough to be heard in the hall where two maids were leaning against the library door, in an attempt to catch every syllable.

Mary grimaced at Anne's language and was about to reprimand her when her daughter started to cry, a wrenching sob that came from deep within her chest and was pitiful to hear.

Mary shook her head in despair. Anne was so lovely, so learned, but so very adamant that she wanted to marry for love. How natural and yet how impossible given the dictates of the Crown. Now each sob that came from Anne's chest was like an arrow piercing her mother's heart. Mary could not bear to listen to such anguish. She wanted to cover her ears to stop the sobs from penetrating to her very core. There was too much sorrow in her life already; she could not bear anymore.

"Anne, I will promise you this. You will not have to marry someone you do not love."

"Really, Mama? Really?"

Anne's head shot up, her sobs stopped immediately, and she leaned over to her mother, hugging her tightly.

"You promise? You can not say this unless you really mean it."

"Yes, Anne. I promise. We will find a way around it."

"Thank you, Mama. Thank you. I know you will never go back on your word for you have always said, 'A promise is a sacred oath.'" The tears of unhappiness that had been streaking down her pale white face immediately became tears of joy.

"My heart is so light I could skip" and she did, out the door and down the hall, almost bumping into a maid who was tiptoeing away. Her steps seemed to echo back the words, "I promise, I promise, I promise."

Mary, sat now alone in the room where she spent every free moment reading and writing—a room whose contents could reveal the wisdom of the ages, but could not reveal to her a way out of Anne's dilemma. The countess shivered with dread at what she just agreed to. *How easy it was for Anne to outfox me,* she mused. *I have made her happy for the moment, but if she persists on this course, her fate is doomed.* She sank back into the carved walnut chair, feeling its hardness and inflexibility. *I should have been just as hard and inflexible,* she thought. She was already ruing her promise.

How to change Queen Elizabeth's mind; that was Mary's dilemma. Elizabeth was nothing if not headstrong in how she ruled England. She exerted total control, even to the point of refusing every eligible suitor for herself, since marrying any one of them might diminish her own power. Mary had used her own power, the power of her pen to write plays with strong, wise, clever women characters, who were loyal to their sex and virtuous to God. She had Juliet ignore her father's wishes and plan to marry Romeo, Hermia in *A Midsummer's Night Dream* did the same; the Princess of France and her ladies in *Love's Labor's Lost* demanded that men show through meditation, good deeds, and celibacy that they were worthy to take a wife. But writing about strong and clever women in plays in seventeenth century England was not the same as actually changing the queen's mind. Elizabeth wanted to have the power to reign as she pleased, but she was not willing to allow other women to control their own destinies.

Mary again considered her daughter's choices with regard to marriage. Anne might claim to be ill, but that was only a temporary out, a delaying tactic. The queen was old and in ill health. At age sixty-seven, she had been on the throne for forty-one years and was the oldest British monarch to date. Maybe if Anne was able to put off an unwelcome marriage until the queen died, the next monarch might approve of a husband closer to her age. If not, there was only one possible way for Anne to avoid marrying an aging widower, but it would cause Mary such great pain that she immediately put it out of her mind. For now, Mary would tell Her Highness that Lady Anne Herbert was sick and confined to her bed.

Chapter Three

December 1600

Wilton House

Musical Codes, Vanishing Ink, and Other Secrets

A knock on the library door startled Mary. "I never seem to get a moment's peace," she muttered. "Come in." A servant entered, bowed low, and announced that her guests had arrived.

"Mercy o' me! They are here already? Time has devoured my morning."

She had forgotten that she was entertaining members of her family and close friends for the next several days. Any communication of Anne's latest "illness" would have to wait. Lady Mary Sidney had company to feed, house, and entertain. She checked her sleeves to see if any ink had spattered on her silk gown or smudged her sleeves above the removable cuffs. Normally she did not go to her library to write just before visitors were expected, but today she decided she needed to edit a scene in a play. She reread the lines scratched on the top page. Before her was a comedy about wives outsmarting a man. Her husband's theatre troupe was to perform it in a few days' time and the actors needed to have their lines memorized.

She leaned back and hit her head on a large tome sticking out from its perch. She reached behind her, pulling the book off the shelf, and ran her fingers over the smooth brown leather cover of Tarlton's *News Out of Purgatory,* which she had been using as a source for her next play. No wonder that she had not put it back properly. There was no room on the shelves since every space was crammed with books from all over Europe, some written in Latin, Greek, French, Italian, Spanish, and Welsh, all languages she had studied as a young girl. There were over three thousand books on literature, history, science, religion, and medicine, some which had come from her parents' library after their deaths in 1586.

She shuddered. *What a horrible year that was. First my parents and then my brother, all dying within months of each other. Ah, poor Philip! Only thirty-two years old but already known as a literary genius.* His passing was the hardest to accept. His death from injuries in a stupid war with Spain still angered Mary, but after a two-year period of mourning for him, she vowed to pick up his mantle, and to write the literature that he would never complete. But what he was allowed to write and publish was not permitted to her, a woman. Her abilities and desires were hemmed in by traditions and laws that made no sense. Sometimes she deeply regretted being born a female.

A voice interrupted her reverie.

"Excuse me, M'Lady. Where shall I ask the guests to wait?"

"God's me. I am distracted this morning. Show them to the corner room, Albert. Tell them I will be there shortly."

Gathering up her papers, Mary looked them over and put one aside. *I will bring this poem to show them,* she thought. *I am sure they will have brought some excellent verse as well.* As she left her library, her worry about Anne's future was pushed aside and she breathed deeply as she made her way down the long hall and into the corner room. That was a delightful space in which she enjoyed entertaining her special guests, mostly members of her literary academy known as The Wilton Circle. The walls were covered with red and gold damask paper, over which hung numerous religious paintings by Italian and Dutch masters. The ceiling was bordered by thick white cornices with classical scenes filling in the area overhead and large glazed windows looked out onto a formal garden. Everywhere the eye gazed there was beauty.

She had invited many of her favorites: Ben Jonson, poet and playwright; her brother Robert, now the Earl of Leicester; Walter Raleigh and Sir John Davies, noted authors; Samuel Daniel, poet and tutor to her children; Nicholas Breton, poet; John Florio, writer. Lady Anne had joined them as well, loving poetry as much as her mother did.

The men stood up and bowed while the ladies curtsied. Mary took her seat at the center of the gathering and after exchanging gossip, she took up her violin and bow and said, "Just this morning I composed a melody and have sent it to Lord Beaufort. Let me play it for you."

As Mary played her violin, her audience listened with rapt attention. When she finished, the room resounded in applause.

"Madam, that piece is the loveliest music I have ever heard," Mr. Daniel gushed.

"It is nothing, just a short composition."

"Anne tells us," Mr. Daniel continued, "that you have recently completed a musical code where each letter of the alphabet is represented by a particular measure and the code can only be broken by reading the written score and using the key to decipher it."

"Yes, it's just a way to amuse myself."

Ben Jonson broke in.

"Now you are mimicking some of my sonnets, in which I give double meanings to words. But you do it in music. I fear you will outwit us all. What other tricks do you have up your sleeve?"

"No doubt you have heard about my disappearing ink that can only be seen when the manuscript it is written on is put over a flame."

"How clever. I swear you would make a first-class spy. So many secrets!"

Mary blushed and lowered her eyes. *If they only knew,* she thought.

"Some secrets must remain hidden, at least for a while." Then looking up, she said, "I do spend many hours in my greenhouse experimenting with plants and chemicals. Adrian Gilbert is there now, assisting me. Tomorrow you must all come and see my potions."

"You are a woman of many talents. And what is it that you are writing now? A sonnet, perhaps?"

"A short poem, but I have just received a new play for Pembroke's Men to perform when they arrive on Saturday. It is about women who get the better of men. You are all invited to come and see it performed. Mr. Breton, what have you been writing?"

"I have brought you a gift—a poem in praise of flowers that I dedicate to you."

"Please, Sir. Read it to us."

"As you wish."

"On a hill there grows a flower,

Fair befall the dainty sweet,

By that flower is a bower

Where the heavenly Muses meet…"

And so each guest present offered a creative piece of writing to be enjoyed and judged by the others. Mary thrived on such an assembly of learned, artistic, and inquisitive confidantes. She, along with the others, enjoyed their position in the world and knew enough to keep each other's secrets, if only to protect their own.

The next day Mary and her guests gathered in a long room with south-facing windows along its entire length. To have that many windows in any room was very expensive but, to Mary, very necessary for they allowed in enough light for plants and flowers to germinate and bud under controlled conditions.

"Come, everyone, and gather around this table. As you can see, my greenhouse is also a laboratory where Mr. Gilbert and I experiment with chemicals and minerals. We have been attempting to change base metal into gold, but so far, we have failed."

"Let us know when you succeed, and we will come with wheelbarrows and chests to help you dispose of it," whispered her brother, in a conspiratorial manner, loud enough for the others to hear.

"I am sure you will, Robert, along with everyone else in England."

Mary saw one of her maids carrying in a large bag.

"Take care, Susan, that you do not spill the bismuth. Bring it here. Now I want you to watch as I mix in some salt with this bismuth and there! Disappearing ink. It has many uses, especially in war and in secret trysts. Let us go into the house to play a game I invented. I will teach you how to remember long lists of numbers forwards and backwards. It will amaze your friends as long as you keep the method a secret."

A cry came from outside, along with the barking of dogs.

"Oh, it is almost time for a hunt. Another day then. I will remain in the house in case my husband is in need of me. The butlers and maids will show you to your rooms so that you can change into proper attire. I will await your return and join you for dinner."

After her guests left for a hunt, Mary, whose husband had been bed-ridden for many months, felt duty-bound to keep close by and retreated to her sewing room where her maids were engaged in needlepoint and embroidery. She checked each girl's handiwork, and then picked up her own cloth. As she stitched, she instructed them.

"Make certain that the threads are pulled with the same dint so the piece will look regular and flat. Priscilla, have your children learned their prayers?"

"Not yet, M'Lady. They are still young."

"You must say a prayer out loud with them morning and night. They will learn quickly that way. All children repeat what they hear, whether good or evil, so we must make them hear good thoughts."

A servant entered the room, flushed with excitement.

"Pardon me, M'Lady. Dame Parker is here to see you. She says it is most urgent."

"Have her wait in the servants' quarters. I will be with her directly. My tenants seem to be in great need of my guidance every day."

Mary walked swiftly to the door that led to the back stairs and into the kitchen. There she found young Nancy Parker, looking disheveled and distraught, wringing her apron. The young woman curtsied quickly, and then began a torrent of speech that sounded like bird chatter.

"Nancy, I do not understand a word. Tell me slowly what has happened."

"My baby is sick. The fever. He just lies there with glassy eyes, staring. What can I do?"

"Go back to him and put cold cloths on his forehead. I will ask Dr. Moffett to look at him directly. Go, go. Your child needs you."

Mary retraced her steps to the hall, and then climbed the grand stairs to her husband's chambers, where he had taken to his bed. In his sixty-seventh year and growing weaker each day, he was fast approaching his final hour. She feared what would happen if he died before her son William was twenty-one, and legally old enough to take charge of his father's estate. Henry Herbert lay moaning in his bed, his arm over a basin where Dr. Moffett, the estate physician since long before Mary had wed Henry, was monitoring the flow of blood from the cut he had made. The doctor was nearly as old as his patient, and his hands shook as he bandaged the jagged cut. His watery eyes, pale cheeks, and scaly skin provided ample testimony to his own poor health. Mary wondered who would die first, the patient or his doctor.

"Good doctor, when you are finished here, there is a tenant whose son is sick with fever. I would like you to attend him."

"I am nearly done." He sighed heavily, exhausted from ministering to this lord nearly at the end of his life and now being asked to look at a babe at the beginning of his. There was to be no rest for him today.

"He will sleep now as I have given him strong wine. All we can do is hope."

"Yes, the miserable have no other medicine but hope."

Mary returned to her sewing, but she could not concentrate. She had been thinking of writing another play, this one about a prince who is grieved by the loss of his dead father and his mother's hasty remarriage to his uncle. She had several acquaintances in mind on whom she would base the characters: William Cecil, otherwise known as Lord Burghley, as the pompous advisor to the king, and two young Danish students, friends of her niece's husband, as the friends of the prince. Of course, she had to disguise the characters enough so that the comparisons would not be obvious.

She left the maids to their stitching and hurried back to her writing desk, hoping she could spend a few hours there without being disturbed. She had written many works—translations, sonnets, ballads, and even explanations of how she wrote in code, a recipe for disappearing ink, and a mnemonic device for remembering long strings of numbers, but her most serious and secret passion was writing plays. She had now written eleven, including history, comedy, and tragedy, and they had become very popular with the theater-goers in England, princes and paupers alike. It had been in her training, in her heritage, in her bones to write powerful, eloquent works that had the power to make people laugh and cry, wonder and believe, pity and admire the characters she could portray just using mere words, some rich in historical references and some created out of her fertile imagination. The body of works she produced was her tribute to her brother Philip who had made it his ambition to elevate the English language with poetry and prose that rivaled the Greek and Roman classics, but died too soon to see his vision realized. Only time would tell if she had achieved that ambition.

Chapter Four

January 1601
Wilton House
A Widow's Constraints

"I fear he will not last the night. He has so many ailments that wrack his body. At sixty-six years, he must be tired."

"Aye, M'Lady. There is much to grieve."

Mary and the doctor's assistant were standing over the bedstead of Lord Henry Herbert, who was barely able to emit a cough. His head seemed to have grown larger and his nose more prominent as his body withered away. His emaciated skeleton was hidden by his night clothes that now swallowed him up.

"Ah, here comes Dr. Moffett. Is there any hope, good Doctor?"

Dr. Moffett came into the chamber, breathing heavily from the exertion of walking up a flight of stairs. He bowed to Lady Sidney, and then bent over to examine Lord Henry Herbert. The doctor lifted up the night shirt and pressed his own gnarled hands on the wrinkled skin of Henry's belly. The Count of Pembroke, once a powerful figure with wealth and lands to rival all other English nobility, groaned in pain and tried to raise his leg, and when he did, the skin on his shin draped down.

He collapsed back into the feather bed, moaning "Let me be" as he closed his rheumy eyes to rest.

"He lacks the will to live. I fear your lord's long struggle is nearly over."

Mary sighed heavily. "Death comes by inches."

"Your husband has lived a long and full life. Your oldest son will inherit a large and prosperous estate."

Mary thought about William, not quite twenty-one so not old enough to take over the duties of his dying father but ambitious enough to obtain, at any price, a great office at Court. Her second son, Philip, just sixteen, handsome and suave, had little inheritance and lacked diligence and patience, but more than made up for those character faults by his wit and charm. He excelled in outdoor activities, like hunting and falconry, but shunned books and lived lavishly like his purse had no bottom. The two brothers were both headstrong in their desire to live the life they wanted, without regard to family or noble directives. Mary's disappointment in both her sons was more pronounced when she compared them to her daughter. Anne's refined tastes in literature and music, her social graces, and her beauty made her most desirable for a wife, but she was dutiful up to a point. It was her determination not to marry the queen's choice for a husband that convinced Mary, Anne would only obey her own soul.

Henry Herbert died later that day, freeing him from the duties and obligations of running his estate, and effectively transferring them to his wife until William reached his majority.

For now, Lord Herbert's enormous land holdings were Mary's to oversee for the next few months until William came of age. She was up to the task but was unaware how much would change when she became a widower. Several weeks later, when the tenants in Cardiff refused to pay their rent, knowing full well that a dowager countess had no clout,

Mary turned to William for advice for she was just beginning to realize how truly powerless a female was in the position of landlady.

"What am I to do about getting the people in Cardiff to pay their due?"

William shrugged and said, "It's not my affair. You handle it. I have to be seen among powerful men in order to keep Father's titles."

Although most of Lord Henry's castles and lands were willed to young William, the offices that Henry had been given by Queen Elizabeth were not automatically transferred to the next-in-line.

"If I do not ingratiate myself to Elizabeth, I will not be considered for powerful positions. That means I must spend every day, watching and waiting for the right opportunities to come along."

"But perhaps if you went to Cardiff and spoke on my behalf, and as your late father's son, the tenants might pay their rents."

"Mother, I am not interested in spending my time on such petty matters. I want to advance my standing with people in power, and in order to do that, I must be seen among them, not in some remote region of England, dealing with illiterate peasants."

"This estate will be yours soon, and then you will have no choice but to attend to its affairs."

"No. I will send others to do that. It is beneath my rank to deal directly with tenants. I only have to wait until our thankless Queen dies, and then my prospects will improve."

Mary smiled grimly. "Yes, your prospects must improve. Elizabeth imprisoned you for impregnating her maid of honor; I tore my hair out at your dishonor. Now you are banished from Court and still you refuse to help me. What further mischief will you do to dishonor your family?"

"Mother, do not meddle in my affairs. I am bound and determined to have a great office bestowed on me, and it will not happen if I remain constrained in this provincial setting."

Mary thought of who else she could turn to. She needed the help of powerful men to bring the rebellious tenants to submit, noblemen for whom the Sidney and Herbert families were as close as cousins. William Cecil, Lord Burghley, was one such acquaintance. He gave her promises, but little else. She went to the Star Chamber, the highest court in England and filed a complaint against some citizens of Cardiff who had destroyed part of her castle wall, beaten her servants, and even arrested a few of them. But a woman alone did not an army make. It all came to naught. Her world was falling apart while her oldest son and heir to his father's fortune was preening at court and her second son was playing at cards.

Chapter Five

March 1603
Cardiff
Elizabeth's Death and Mary's Despair

More than two years after Sir Henry Herbert died, his oldest son and heir to his estate still had not become involved in its management. He had left the day-to-day running of it in the hands of his capable mother, Lady Mary Sidney, leaving it to her to bring their tenants to heel. The widow and her still unmarried daughter stood by the windows in one of their castles in Cardiff, staring at the harsh Welsh landscape, both angry that they had to come so far on what seemed to be a fruitless task.

"Mother, I don't see why William doesn't come here to collect rents and settle disputes. Cardiff is part of his inheritance and therefore his responsibility."

"Please, Anne. Do not bother me with complaints. To mend his behavior is hopeless. He pretends to be a lord, but he is just a fool. He thinks that an estate this size will take care of itself. No matter. He will get his due afore God."

"You have also called Philip a fool."

"Yes, he does nothing but talk of his horse. Both your brothers vex me. They do not act as if they know what is expected of them. And you, Anne, by refusing to marry whomever the queen chooses for you, are putting yourself in danger. I am at my wit's end to procure a marriage that will please both you and Elizabeth." As she spoke, she paced up and down the icy cold room of Cardiff Castle where neither the pitifully meager flames of the fireplace nor the decorated arras hanging on the wall could remove the chill in her bones. The utter bleakness of this late winter's morning was depressing her energy and spirit. Anne tried once more to defend her position regarding marriage.

"Mother, I have seen firsthand what little happiness comes from marrying an old man. My father was already graying when I was born. He regarded me as an annoyance. When I became a young girl, he assumed me to be weak and foolish and so he had nothing to say to me, except to complain that he had to provide for a dowry when I married. He once said he wished I were a boy. How I wish that also."

"Wishing is for fools. You have the mind of a general and heart of a tiger. That will carry you far."

Mary looked down at the pile of papers on her desk and took an account book in her hand, opening it to a marked page. She shook her head in dismay.

"There are so many unpaid rents this quarter. Do these tenants think they can squat on the lord's lands for nothing? Do I need to bring an army with me to show teeth to these freeloaders?"

There was a loud knock on the door and a servant rushed in.

"Mi'Ladies, a messenger has come from London with terrible news."

"Show him in. It is never good to bring bad news."

A plump, red-faced herald, wild-eyed and covered with dust, appeared at the door, bowed to the countess and blurted out, "Our beloved Queen is dead!"

"Mercy o'me!" Mary made the sign of the cross and, bowing her head, murmured a prayer for Elizabeth's soul. "Our queen has at last succumbed to her illnesses. I pray her end was quick. We must leave here with all due speed. First to Wilton for proper dress, and then to London for her funeral. A monarch dead with no progeny! Alas, these are trying times. God save us all."

"Who will be crowned next, Mother? A Protestant or a Catholic?"

"I pray it is a Protestant, and most likely, her Scottish cousin James, who has sway in Parliament. That won't please the Catholics, but if he is clever, he will let the Catholics be. They are in great numbers and can cause trouble, by heaven. Now we must away to Wilton House. The queen will be buried within a month, and there is much to do."

The next day the entourage of noblewomen, servants, and hangers-on made their way by carriage along the bumpy and sometimes muddy dirt roads from Cardiff to Wiltshire, just outside of Salisbury, a distance of about seventy miles. Traveling a top speed, it took them five long days before the tower above the north facade of the large mansion appeared in the distance.

It was a welcome sight, but the countess could not remain home for long. Mary, along with her three children—William, Philip, and Anne—prepared for the ninety-mile journey to London. They needed to arrive there well before the funeral procession in order to learn their roles in the extravagant pomp and ceremony expected to be given any royal monarch, dead or alive. As queen, Elizabeth had travelled from her court to castles and manor houses all over England, intent upon having herself seen and handing out favors to peasants in an effort to make her countrymen love her. It had worked. The people of England, almost to a man, cheered whenever Elizabeth appeared before them.

Now, as the Sidney train wound its way through the English countryside, they encountered nobles, yeoman, farmers, and peasants all heading in the same direction. They had loved having a queen who travelled by their plot of land, or had stayed in their master's house, or had thrown sweets to them as her carriage passed by. Elizabeth knew how to attract the goodwill of her people, and they took the bait.

But Mary's son, William, had no love for the queen. Elizabeth had briefly imprisoned and then banished him from court for getting one of her attendants, Lady Mary Fitton, pregnant. Now, in preparation for the queen's funeral, Lady Mary pleaded with Lord Chamberlain George Carey, who was overseeing the funeral procession, to overlook this shame and give William the honor to help carry the banner of England in the long march from Whitehall to Westminster Abbey. He reluctantly agreed, and both William and his brother Philip, distant cousins to Elizabeth, moved in lockstep along the broad streets of London, wearing the distinctive blue and yellow Sidney colors. It was a proud moment for Mary, and as disgusted as she was with William's immoral behavior, she held out hope that he had learned his lesson and would henceforth behave honorably and help her govern the estate that was now his.

But it was not to be. When Mary was at Wilton House preparing for the elaborate funeral, she sent her jewels and money on ahead with a trusted servant. The servant was accosted, robbed, and beaten so severely that he eventually died from his wounds. When the attacker was caught and brought to trial, he argued that Mary was a hysterical woman of no standing. Mary had begged William to appear with her in court, but he had refused. Hence Mary stood alone in the Star Chamber, without the support of any male figure, listening to the defense ridiculing her claim. She was certain that her word would be given more weight over that of a known thief. But without either of her sons there to speak on her behalf, the judges took the word of a known embezzler and cheat over hers, a titled woman and widow to a lord whose land holdings were immense. The case was thrown out.

Mary left the civil court, embarrassed and shaken by the treatment she received. She grumbled, "William forgets how I interceded to have him released from prison, how I managed to convince Carey to give him a prominent role at Elizabeth's funeral, and yet when I plead my case to the judges, he is not there to strengthen my arguments. The judges showed me no mercy."

She staggered to her carriage for the long ride back to Wilton House, feeling as if her world had been lost to her when her husband died. Her thoughts were of what the future held.

"I know who I am, but not what I may become. How far I have fallen. A wife without a husband is like a cart without a horse. Useless."

Chapter Six

May 1603
Wiltshire
The Wilton Circle

It was a sunny May day when a group of writers gathered in the grand salon at Wilton House. Their purpose in coming there was to discuss their own poetic verses and to denigrate the unworthy scribblings of the charlatans who wrote doggerel or even worse, pirates who put their names on the works of others. They had little patience with the imitators or outright thieves of what they considered proper poetry.

Seated next to Lady Mary Sidney, the hostess and titular head of this illustrious gathering, was Michael Drayton a prolific writer, who first became noticed when he wrote *Idea: The Shepherd's Garland.* More recently he had composed a series of sonnets that had gained wide, popular appeal. Drayton was not a regular attendee at these gatherings, and so was not aware of Mary's involvement in writing plays for the stage. Samuel Daniel knew. He was a close friend of Mary's, and was in the seat of honor, across from her. Edmund Spenser had praised Daniel's book of poems *Delia,* and Daniel's reputation as a writer soared. One very familiar person, Fluke Greville, had travelled the farthest to be with them on this day. Mary had insisted that he attend because Fluke and her brother Philip had traveled the Continent together years ago and had become so supportive of Mary's writings, that he became her mentor and confidante. Sir Robert Sidney, Mary's brother, and his daughter Lady Mary Wroth, both occasional poets, came because they enjoyed being in the company of more celebrated writers of verse. They both were in the dark about Mary's secretive works which meant that those who knew had to keep their own comments in check. Lastly, there sat Mary's daughter Anne, knowing her mother's secret as well as having some herself.

"I regret that Sir Edmund Spenser is no longer with us. His works, especially *A Shepherd's Complaint,* were brilliant. How untimely was his death at forty-seven years of age." Fulke Greville shook his head sadly. "Such a pity."

"Yes. I think of him and Philip often, both dying while their minds were so fertile. They were the fairest flowers of our time," bemoaned Lady Mary. "All the more reason to write as much as we can while we can."

Samuel Daniel nodded his assent. "No one can fault you for not writing enough. I have never seen you without a pile of vellum on your desk ready to be filled with a poem or letter, even while you are entertaining half of England."

Lady Mary laughed lightly and tried to steer the conversation away from her own works. "I would rather be ambitious than live idly in the sun. But you are not my only guests this day. The Pembroke Players are here to perform and with them is Master Shakespeare."

"Ah, the playwright ." Daniel looked at Mary with raised eyebrows, as if to warn her where this conversation was leading.

" What I don't understand," continued Drayton, "is where Shakespeare learned about courtly life and military matters. The history plays discuss such topics in a very familiar way. He certainly did not ascertain such information from other actors."

"Or his references to female pursuits, like cooking, sewing, and taking care of babes. His plays are full of references to such things," rejoined Lady Wroth.

"And yet no other poet has come forth to challenge his claim as author," exclaimed Drayton. "And so he continues to attach his name as editor or author."

"Yes, that bothers me, too," said Lord Robert.. I am glad some of us here don't take Shakespeare at his word."

"Another subject on which he seems to have great authority is the law," Lady Mary Wroth put in. "There are several plays—*The Merchant of Venice,* for one—in which he shows a substantial knowledge of court proceedings."

"Perhaps he appeared in court as a plaintiff," Fluke Greville suggested.

"Or as a defendant," declared Lady Mary Wroth.

"Have you noticed how women are portrayed in his plays? They are all strong, principled, and clever. Nary a one displays weakness. And when pitted against men, they use trickery and their feminine wiles to best them. Shakespeare must hold women in high regard," continued Lord Robert.

"And yet," Drayton countered, "I heard stories from different quarters about his womanizing. That doesn't fit with his depictions of them in his plays."

"You are right," Robert affirmed. "I hear he frequently is seen at The Tavern outside London where he enjoys the pleasures of the owner's wife. That should certainly put to rest his high opinion of women."

Throughout this discussion, Lady Mary Sidney listened intently but offered no particular thoughts on the matter. She let the visitors ramble on as they wished, waiting to see how the question of Shakespeare's intimate familiarity with such a wide array of topics would end.

"Well, I certainly could not write so well on all those subjects," stated Samuel Daniel. "It would take not only a mind of the highest quality but a nature that was observant and introspective."

"And also a poet who is able to produce excellent works at an astounding pace," added Robert Sidney. "Mary, you are the only person I know who writes constantly and yet you show us only a smattering of your writings."

"Alas, Brother," replied Mary. "Some of my writings are of a personal nature. Be content with what I do show you. As for the man Shakespeare, he stayed here a while when the Lord Chamberlain's Men came to perform earlier this year. Burbage showed his skills as an actor in the role as Caesar, and Shakespeare held his own in one of the minor roles, Lucilius, I believe."

"No, I am sure you are wrong. I was there. He played Messala," said her brother, gently correcting her.

"You are right," Lady Mary agreed. "A passing performance but not memorable."

"When you spoke to Shakespeare," asked Drayton, "did he exhibit any great knowledge in the areas we have discussed?"

Lady Mary paused. "No, he seemed courteous and affable. We exchanged pleasantries and remarks on acting. Nothing more."

"Did he offer any poem, any sonnet he wrote for your perusal? He must know of Wilton Circle."

"I did extend an invitation to him to join us in our discussions, but he declined, saying that time would not permit it."

Drayton pressed on. "He must have a library of hundreds of books and is able to read in several languages in order to write plays taken from Italian, Latin, French, and Greek sources. That fits the description of a nobleman's education, not an actor's. No commoner could write so extensively. Of course, he may not have written them at all but is putting his name on the title page, stealing the plays like a pirate steals treasure. My own works as well as Raleigh's have been printed under someone else's name without our permission."

"What should an author do if he has written sublime poetry or prose but cannot publish under his own name?" the countess asked in an off-hand way. "Why must he keep his brilliance hidden and his works turned to dust? Surely, a work that is published anonymously or under the name of a beard does not alter its beauty?"

"So," said her brother Robert, "you are arguing to have anonymous works allowed to be published for their intrinsic value to the world?"

"Precisely."

"But, Mary, if a work is of such high quality, why wouldn't the author who is paying to have it published, do so with his name boldly written on the front and receive the acclaim he deserves?"

"Perhaps his position in society or the argument he puts forth within its pages forbids it," she responded.

"That is unfortunate, but he must wait for another time or king who would allow it. Those who are ahead of their times must suffer the curse of having to abide by the laws and customs under which they live."

"And in the meantime, the printers behave exactly like pirates—stealing what is not theirs for profit. A crime by any measure," said Lady Mary Wroth. "The Crown should put a stop to it."

"Where there is money to be made, there will always be men who will risk punishment to make a profit. I fear it is unstoppable," responded her father.

"An eloquent author, although banned by the Crown, will find ways to circumvent the law," replied Lady Mary Sidney. "Great works can never be suppressed."

She prayed her words would prove true.

Chapter Seven

Fall 1604

Wilton House

Illicit Sex and Ignoble Secrets

"King James has agreed to see me and hear me plead my case to be Lord Chamberlain. With that title, my greatest wish will be fulfilled."

Lady Mary and her son William were standing in a large drawing room at Wilton House, keeping their distance from each other, like two combatants sizing the other up. Mary looked radiant in a dark blue silk gown, with a wide band of lacy ruff and a long, white, double pearl necklace hanging from her neck. On top of her red curly hair sat a white lace headpiece. Although she had been a widow for the last three years, she was determined to keep up the appearance and the power of her illustrious ancestry. Today she was going to sit for a portrait artist and she wanted to reflect the height of fashion in 1604, by looking every inch an English noblewoman. For her entire life, she had been a welcome guest in the royal court and even spent many Christmas dinners at Elizabeth's table. Her new status as a dowager countess held no sway in the court of King James, but apparently her eldest son's stature was not diminished, being a regular at court. He was dressed in fashionable rich brown silk waistcoat, doublet and breeches, stockings with embroidered satin at the ankle, and, for good measure, a gold chain with an emerald pendant. At that moment, both were attempting to display righteous and judicious conduct despite rumors to the contrary. William's words oozed with smugness and satisfaction.

"I pray that my expected appointment will please you, Mother. You cursed me for my having an affair with Mary Fitton, and then railed at me for marrying Mary Talbot. I hope once I am appointed to this position, it will prove to you how little my previous behavior has mattered."

His self-serving analysis intended to show that his mother's fears for his future at Court of King James were baseless. Mary thought otherwise.

"By any measure, your behavior has been most dishonorable."

"Don't lecture me on dishonor. You who consort with the new doctor, a commoner, so soon after my father died. You who write maudlin verse and bawdy plays in hugger-mugger while you pretend to be a pious Christian. Tell me, which one of us is the more honest?"

Mary was taken aback by his accusations about her behavior. She wanted to stop up her ears. How wretched to have a thankless child who denied his personal wrongdoing while twisting the meaning of her own actions. She matched his taunts with those of her own.

"You may be honest, but you are not honorable, not when you refused to marry a woman who carried your child. Not when you leave me on my own to do battle with upstart tenants. Have you no regard for your father's estate or your mother's prospects?"

"My ambitions are to be met at court, not in places of little influence and power. You handle the complaints about the tenants."

"I have tried to deal with the tenants, but I was met with hostility and disdain. What am I now? Just an old woman with no more power than a chambermaid. A woman, no matter her title or respectability, has no chance to be triumphant against her subjects in such a world."

The injustice of it all infuriated her. Her son was berating her for her conduct with Dr. Lister, the estate's new physician and a welcomed confidant, and for writing words that brought audiences to shed tears or shake with laughter when, at the same time, he was refusing to fulfill his duties as a landlord. Mary's disposition, up to this point—controlled and confidant—changed suddenly, like a fighter backed into a corner. Her chin went up, and she turned to face her opponent with her only weapon available—her wits. She had suffered so many indignities since her husband died. Rebuffed by tenant farmers who had dutifully paid their rents in the past, maligned by the Star Court as being balmy, and disparaged by her own son for her kindness and affections to the estate's doctor, she turned to glare at him with such an anger that she didn't believe she possessed. How dare her son question her behavior when he, himself, was a favorite of a degenerate king. Mary had heard ugly stories regarding King James and his love of young, handsome men. Undone by William's cutting remarks, she let loose with a tirade of blasphemies.

"You have the moral resolve of a whore. I have heard that you are spending much time in shameful behavior with our immoral king. That is not the behavior that I expect from my eldest son, heir to his father's fortunes and good name."

William's face turned red. He took a step toward her, pointed his finger at her, and bellowed, "You dare to call my behavior immoral? You, who after Dr. Moffett died, dare to consort with the new doctor. You, who write sonnets and plays that do not befit a woman. You, who lie to the king about your daughter's health so she can escape a royally ordained marriage. I do not regard those things as acceptable behavior from my mother! You cannot deny any part of what I say."

Mary's face flushed with embarrassment, and she turned her face away to try to hide her shame. The drawing room in which they were standing was connected to the main hall by two doors, both of which had been left open. The walls seemed to reverberate with his accusations and travel out into the hall, where there were certain to be maids listening.

"Hold your tongue," she whispered, in a trembling voice. "The servants will hear you. Dr. Lister is a learned gentleman and a friend. My relationship with him is perfectly proper."

William stood with his hands on his hips, threw his head back, and roared with laughter. He wagged his finger at her just as she had done to him when he was a bad little boy. Mary cringed, humbled but defiant. Her voice rose as she tried to shift the argument.

"And do not chide me for my versifying. I have seen how you revel in watching the plays. You enjoy them as much as the Court and commoners do. My writings are what keep me from going mad with sorrow over the deaths I have suffered, first Catherine who was only three, then later my father, mother, and brother, all within a few months. I use my pen to pour out my grief or to bring some joy to a cruel world. It cannot be wrong to use a God-given gift. The queen herself asked for more comedies. Ben Jonson spoke of the playwright as having a silvered tongue."

Mary's face broke into a slight smile. She could not help herself. What a compliment from such a notable poet, even though he knew not who the true author was.

"That does not exonerate you from your sins, Mother, but only reflects on your impure disposition. It is not permitted for a woman to write lusty verses."

"Do not judge me on my disposition, until you but look in a mirror. As for Anne, she wants only what you have been allowed to do, marry a person of her own choosing. Your father was three times my age and had no spirit left to practice husbandly or fatherly duties. I will not permit such heartbreak on Anne. It is you who bring shame on this family. You whose defects taint the Herbert lineage. You who make mockery of decency and decorum."

William was not to be quieted.

"Don't you dare tell me how to behave when you act more like a strumpet than a countess. I have seen how you take the doctor's arm and whisper in his ear. How you kneel in church and bow your head in prayer and all the time you are conjuring up bawdy plays and for what purpose? Titillation? Bravado? If your secrets were ever found out, my reputation would be tarnished forever."

"Your own actions have already tarnished your reputation. My writings will stay secret unless you divulge their true authorship. I have intervened on your behalf; I have abased myself before Elizabeth and her Court to obtain your release from prison. And what is my reward? Puffery and petulance! Enough! I wish I could chuck you out like the offal from a slaughtered sheep."

They had been standing in shadow between two windows. Now the light from the morning sun moved over them, exposing their figures in a garish glare for anyone to see. It made both of them uncomfortable, and they immediately moved back into the shade. The dam, long strained from the pressures of staying civil, had fractured and there was no repairing it. The secrets that each had tried to keep from the other had burst forth and spread across the room like a tsunami, engulfing them in a flood of rage. Finally, William broke the silence.

"No need to chuck me out, Mother. I am leaving. As long as you debase this house, I will never step foot in it again."

William strode out of the drawing room and left Wilton House for London and the Court of King James. Mary waited until his footsteps faded and she had regained a calmer bearing. She went immediately to the small chapel at the end of the hall, and knelt before the crucifix to ask God's forgiveness for her distemper and to pray for both their souls. It was a plea without remedy. What she wanted, really wanted, was for her sonnets and plays to be printed for the world to see , or read, and enjoy. She also wanted her daughter to be happily married and for herself to marry again, this time to someone of her own choosing. She laughed at the impossibility of such things ever happening. All three desires involved the power of a woman to control her own life. The times were not in her favor.

Chapter Eight

Summer 1606

Wilton House

Anne Must Die

"Anne, you cannot go! I won't allow it."

Mary had entered Anne's sunlit bedchamber and was watching her daughter try on a new dress of pale green silk with satin bows and a low-cut bodice, part of a costume to be worn for the masque at the Court of King James. It was stunningly beautiful as was her daughter in it.

"Mother, Ben Jonson himself asked me to perform in the masque he has written. There is nothing I love better to do. I must attend and wear this new dress as well."

"But, Anne, who will believe you have been ill when you arrive there in the pink of health? How can I tell everyone that you are still feeling poorly?"

"Fiddlesticks! I care not what people think. I will go to Court and be sick later."

"I pray, Anne, do not make me as mad as a March hare. I will tear my hair out if you continue this prattle. Your only hope in marriage is to obey the king's command. Otherwise, get thee to church and beg for God's mercy. There is no other recourse but a nunnery or death."

"It will never be a nunnery, of that I am certain, for to me, a nunnery is death. I want to marry a handsome young man with a good education—a clergyman or doctor perhaps—, and have an abundance of children, and teach them their letters and encourage them to go out in the world and make their mark, so that in later years, my husband will still be with me to enjoy our offspring."

Lady Mary could only pull at her red curls, now mixed with a little gray, as she listened to such prattle. She despaired for Anne's future. A mournful cry escaped from her throat, and she moaned, "How much sadness and sorrow must I endure?" Mary had intended to remain strong and resolute as she was trained to do, but now she wept bitter tears. Anne rushed over, held her mother close, and kissed her cheek, tasting the salty drops that ran down her mother's face. She was filled with shame.

"I am sorry to cause you such pain, Mama. You have taught me to think for myself, and now I act out of conviction, not duty. Perhaps you have taught me too well."

"My curse is to expect too much from my children. I fear for your future. I see only gloom ahead."

As if on cue, a dark cloud crept across the sun, changing the room's pale pink walls to a somber gray. Mary felt a shudder run down her back, like a premonition, cold and deadly. Leaning back against the bedroom wall, she sagged and tried to steady herself, not wanting to collapse in front of Anne. She took a deep breath and let her emotions settle down. She would not, could not lose another daughter.

Anne did not see the darkness that had swept over her mother. She continued on as if this conversation was like all the others on the subject of her marriage.

"I will pretend to be sick when the occasion suits me. Do you want me to end up like other young, titled ladies who wed much older men, and die while still in their twenties, weakened from conceiving children in rapid succession, or withering away as their beauty fades while their disenchanted husbands have affairs with younger women?"

Lady Mary shook her head and clasped her hands in prayer. She knew that the prospects of Anne having a loving husband were slim. King James I was an outsider at court, having grown up in Scotland, and he needed the support of powerful nobles. If a widower who had land and titles asked him for permission to wed a lovely young noble lady, why should he deny such a union? Mary no longer had a husband to speak for Anne's prospects, and her sons were only interested in what the future held for them. Lady Anne Herbert, as well as all the other people in England, were like pieces on a chess board and could only move in directions that protected the most powerful piece, in this case, the king. What could Mary do?

A few weeks later, a missive came from yet another earl, recently widowed. The unopened letter lay on Mary's desk like a poisonous snake, too dangerous to touch but also too dangerous to ignore. When Mary finally undid the seal, and read its contents, her heart froze. Indeed, another suitor had made his appeal to marry Lady Anne, who was now twenty-three years old and extremely desirable for a bride. The widower in question, Lord Hertford, was almost three times Anne's age. Her daughter had brought attention to herself at the masque, demonstrating to this suitor that she was not ill. She had now refused to marry three previous suitors, and the Crown was becoming suspicious about her bouts with ill health. Time, which had moved at a slow pace, was now at full gallop. Something had to be done and quickly.

In desperation, mother and daughter concocted a plan that, no matter the outcome, would bring sorrow to them both. Within a week, Mary announced that Anne was sick yet again. Together, they left for Cambridge with Dr. Lister in order that Anne might find help for her unspecified illness. Cambridge, England was a city known for its excellent medical treatments and far enough away from London to hide their activities from the king. While they were there, Mary let it be known that Anne had suddenly become very ill. Within a few weeks, Anne was pronounced dead by her doctor. The burial took place in Cambridge, and Mary and Dr. Lister returned to Wilton House with heavy hearts, spreading the sad news to the family and the Court.

Anne had made her choice—self over duty—and now the die had been cast; there was no going back. Mary was at her beads each morning, praying fervently for Anne's soul. Her daughter who had once been a child of good hope was now gone from her forever. How strange it was to walk around her grand house with so many empty rooms. It made her feel all the more insignificant and weak.

She again turned to writing as an outlet for the grief that was consuming her waking hours. A tragedy was appropriate, and the historic chronicle of King Leir and his relationships with his three daughters fit her mood. As she wrote, she imagined herself as Leir (whom she called "Lear") and his offspring as her own children: William and Philip consumed by ambition, and Anne, headstrong and idealistic. In the play, the two older children ingratiate themselves with their parent to cement their inheritance while the youngest one is brutally honest and tells him her love cannot be bought. Too late, King Lear realizes that it was his youngest child who really loved him. Mary likened her older sons to Lear's older daughters who worked to gain more power and wealth, while her youngest child Anne was like Lear's youngest daughter Cordelia who had to be true to herself.

Now her own daughter, Anne was gone from her forever.

Mary had depended on Dr. Lister to find a solution to Anne's plight; his suggestion was trickery in the extreme. It seemed to have worked, and her gratitude was profound. She would be in his debt for the rest of her life. His words of understanding, his support, and his love he gave to her could never be repaid. She was indeed having an affair with her doctor; William had been right all along.

A few weeks later, a letter came addressed to Lady Mary Sidney Herbert. The handwriting was familiar. Mary quickly opened it but saw nothing but one sheet of music written on vellum paper. She hurried to her library and taking up her quill and blank paper, decoded the musical notes. A smile burst forth on her mouth and tears came to her eyes. She left the library and asked a servant where Dr. Lister was.

"I believe he is walking on the grounds, M'Lady. He left only a short while ago."

"Go find him and tell him to come to the library at once."

When Matthew entered the room, Mary waved the sheet of music in the air and whispered, "I have good news." Mary read Matthew the decoded message, both of them elated by its contents.

Messages continued to arrive at monthly intervals—sometimes a sheet of music and sometimes just a blank piece of paper, which Mary placed over a candle, letting the heat of the flame do its work. Slowly, words appeared on the page as if by magic. The inky words remained legible until the heat source was removed and the vellum was again a blank piece of paper. Mary's inventions, at one time thought to be just clever parlor games, became a secret way of communicating with one who could no longer be with her.

Of course, she had to destroy all evidence resulting from using her cunning inventions; if her secrets were found out, the king would unleash his wrath not only on her but also on her children. She could never bring shame, disgrace, and ruin to the long and illustrious history of her family.

She was confident she could outwit the king and live her life on her terms. But she must never, never let her guard down.

BOOK TWO

Sarah Burton and Robert Dudley

Chapter One

October 1607
Somewhere in southwest England
A Stranger by the Door

"Damn this rain," Robert grumbled. "Not only am I wounded and lost, but God is trying to drown me as well."

It had been raining ever since he fled from his attackers. His acute pain made him curse his fate as he tried to hold on to the reins of his horse with one hand and keep his useless left arm close to his chest. Exhaustion added to his troubles. Just keeping his eyes open took considerable effort. *I must have dozed off, but for how long? Ten minutes? An hour?*

His steadfast horse moved slowly over the cold, wet ground. It did not seem to mind the rain pelting down. Again he muttered, this time much louder. "A curse on Essex and the yellow-bellied coward who shot at me without warning. By Jove, I'll whip that fellow until he cries for Satan to rescue him."

A cold wind blew across his body, and he reached down to touch his breeches to be sure he was not naked. The driving rain made it impossible to see anything. Where on earth was he? Again and again, he heard pebbles and stones bounce off his horse's hooves. In his foggy brain a thought occurred to him. *This is a road! People must live nearby.*

As the rain started to let up, a chill shook him, making the throbbing in his arm feel like hammer blows. He wanted to scream, but that would only please his enemies if they were following him. All but one of their bullets had missed. He had tried to bind the wound with his silk scarf, but it was awkward working with only one hand so he used his teeth to hold one end while he knotted it just above the wound. It took a while and he had lost a lot of blood. Now his left arm hung limply by his side. He leaned forward to rest himself on his horse's neck. "I cannot go on. If I do not find help soon, I will bleed to death. Better that I had been shot through the heart," he groused.

Suddenly his horse stopped. Robert tensed. He tried to sit up, but it was too difficult. He looked through half-opened eyes, seeing nothing to his left but woods and fields. The smell of burning wood filled his nostrils. A campfire, perhaps? Ridiculous. Impossible in this weather. He strained to hear, but there was only the cursed wind whipping pebbles across the ground. No amount of nudging the animal's flanks got it to move on. It whinnied, and then snorted. It was trying to tell him something, but what? Did the path end? Was there a precipice ahead? He prayed that whatever it was, it would give him relief from his suffering.

A creak, like a door opening, made him start. His heart leapt. He would soon know his fate. A soft cry reached his ears, and he let out a sigh, then sagged. He felt himself start to slide off his saddle. Moments later, hands were pulling him down. As soon as he touched the ground, he lost consciousness.

Chapter Two

October 1607
The Mews
Sarah's Problem

Sarah Burton stared at the man lying at her feet in the mud. In her twenty-eight years on Earth, she had never seen a man dismount from a horse that way, and a stranger to boot. He had to be drunk. His pale face and sunken cheeks gave him a ghostly expression. She looked at him more closely and saw that he wore leather breeches and a fitted coat of fine cloth. His boots were of smooth brown leather with no wear or mud on them. *That was strange,* she thought. Why would a man who was so well dressed, ride off in the rain after getting drunk instead of spending the night in an inn?

"There is no accounting for what men will do."

She shook her head in disgust. Then Sarah's eye caught sight of the man's left sleeve, which was torn and bloody.

"God's me! He must have injured himself and lost his way." But where had he come from and where was he going? She could not ask her father about this man. Dr. Burton had left for Wells only this morning and would not be back for two days. Sarah realized that she had to care for him by herself. Involuntarily, she reached up and touched the scar on her face, a perpetual reminder of a violent attack many years ago. "I won't allow it to happen again," she vowed.

She suddenly remembered that both she and her unannounced guest were getting soaked. "Mercy! I mustn't spend any more time dawdling. I need to get him inside if I am to help him."

She called to Peter. A sturdy young lad of twelve, with straw-colored hair and well-worn shirt and breeches, came limping from the stable.

"Help me drag this man into the house and take care you do not pull on his left arm."

Sarah lifted the man's shoulders, while Peter put his arms around the man's waist and together they half carried, half dragged the body into the large parlor.

"Let's lay him here by the fire as gently as you can. Peter, have you ever seen this man?"

"No, Miss Sarah. Not on my life."

"Well, he can't be dangerous in his condition. Take his horse into the stable while I attend to this sorry creature."

"Yes, Miss. Shall I wipe down the horse and feed it?"

"Of course, Peter. We must show kindness to both man and beast. And then return. I will need you to help me undress him. His garments are soaked through."

As Sarah hurried to get her father's black medical bag, her thoughts turned back to this stranger. Since he was unknown to her, it meant that he had come from a very long way. Sarah and her father were familiar with everyone for miles around; John Burton's medical practice and his scientific and literary pursuits gave him reason to travel throughout the area. He had visited or entertained nearly every person of note in southwest England, so this body lying on the ground had to have come from the north or east, probably London.

The medical bag had seen better days but still served its purpose. Inside were gauzes, cutting implements, extracts of herbs, and various salves for easing a patient's complaints. She also snatched a pile of clean linen strips from the trestle table that her father used as a desk as well as for examinations. When she knelt next to the still body, her eyes were drawn to his neatly trimmed black beard, and the long, shiny locks of hair encircling his head. He wore no jewelry, but the cut of his garments and his general cleanliness indicated he was a gentleman who took care in his appearance. The growing circle of red just below his left shoulder brought her back to her task. She needed to remove his upper garments in order to treat his wound. The medical bag held scissors that her father had forged himself. She found them and was about to cut away the cloth between his shoulder and the wound when she noticed that the material was silk, but so drenched in blood that it was barely visible from the rest of the sleeve. It was tied above the wound as a tourniquet.

Her first thought was to simply cut it away, but she hesitated. No man she knew owned a silk scarf. *I mustn't destroy it,* she thought. *It might be very dear to him.* Instead she unknotted the silk cloth and set it aside. She unlaced the stitches that attached the sleeve to the rest of the coat, slid the sleeve off his arm, and ripped open the seams of his shirt. Then, taking a clean linen strip and dipping it into the pot of water hanging over the fire, she pressed the cloth around the wound to wash away the blood. To her amazement, she saw a bullet embedded in his arm. She seldom had treated anyone with such an injury, but she knew exactly what to do. A bullet must be removed, and the wound cleaned. She retied the tourniquet, and using her father's thin knife, she deftly removed the bullet. The man's head shook as he let out a loud groan, but he remained unconscious. She poured some wine over the wound to lessen the chance of infection, and then applied figwort to hasten its healing. With steady hands, she stitched the opening and finally removed the tourniquet and wrapped the arm in linen cloths. She had done all she could, she reasoned. If the loss of blood had not been considerable and if the wound did not get infected, the stranger would make a quick recovery.

Peter returned to say that the horse was settled in the stable.

"Good. Now we must remove the rest of his drenched clothes and put warm blankets over him." As she wiped his face and hair, she stared at his angular features and closed eyes. His appearance reminded her of an ascetic that she had seen in a book about Spanish history. Such a strong, noble look hinted at a person of great heritage.

"I wonder what sorry story he will tell."

The man breathed heavily.

"We may not know for quite a while. Peter, he will stay here by the fire for the night. We can try to put him abed in the morning. Jane may be back by then and can help us."

"Is her sister better?" asked Peter.

"Yes. Her fever has gone down, and the worst seems to be over."

After Peter left for his sleeping quarters in the stable, she took the scissors and knife and placed them in a pan of hot water as her father had taught her to do. Then gathering up the bloody clothes and silk scarf, she filled a basin and began to wash them. Her thoughts again returned to this stranger who had appeared out of nowhere. *This house is far from any large town,* she thought. *He must have traveled far.* As she rung out the silk cloth and stretched it to put on the drying rack, her eyes froze on the center design, a blue arrowhead on a gold background. She immediately recognized it as the Sidney family coat of arms. She had seen it on the door of a carriage when she and her father were in London for the funeral of Queen Elizabeth. The Sidney family had immense power with the king and owned large portions of land far to the north of Wells. It was unlikely that the man lying in her parlor had stolen this scarf. His clothes were too fine to be that of a highwayman or even a soldier. Who was he? That question stoked the gathering firestorm in her brain. She loved solving mysteries of any sort, and this stranger qualified as a particularly intriguing one. She decided she must interrogate him when he woke up.

During the night, Sarah's sleep was disturbed several times by groaning from the parlor below. She was tempted to get up from her bed to check on him but decided against it. He was too weak to rise, and all she could do for him was done. If he woke, it would be better he not see her alone and in her night garments.

Chapter Three

October 1607
The Mews
Truths and Half-truths

The sound of the rooster crowing startled Sarah. She had slept poorly, in fits and starts, alert to the creaking of the beams of the house and the patter of mice in the walls. She rose feeling only half awake. After putting on a simple linen smock and waistcoat, she wrapped her long hair around her head with pins. There was a small commonplace mirror on her night table, indistinct in its reflection due to its poor quality. She seldom picked it up, but this morning she did and stared for a long time at her image. Her luminous green eyes, dark red hair, smooth skin tanned by the sun and, of course, the long scar across her left cheek were in blurry focus. She sighed. At twenty-eight, she should have been married with several children. That hope ended long ago. How many years now? Almost fourteen. The scar had gone from bright red to a dull pink, but it was still the first thing strangers looked at when she greeted them. She put the mirror down and promised herself not to look at it again. It did no good to revive hurtful memories. What was done could never be made right. Her face and belly would carry her disfigurement her whole life.

The Mews was where she began her life and surely it was here where she would end it, caring for her father and servants as well as the people in the village. As she moved about the room, she thought of all she had learned from the books and travelers her father had brought home. Some of the journeymen had been to France and beyond. They told fascinating stories, wore beautiful clothes, and sometimes traded books on science and medicine which she read from cover to cover. Their discussions on what they had seen and heard had given her the deepest pleasure she had ever felt. Oh, to be a man with the means to travel the world, to eat exotic foods, to stand before the temples, pyramids, and cathedrals of men's creations, to feast one's eyes on the deserts, mountains, and jungles of nature's wonders. Those grand sights were all unattainable, but Sarah never regretted reading about them. Her uninvited guest downstairs may have seen such sights, though. All the more reason to question him.

She descended the stairs, reviewing what she would say to the figure lying by the fireplace. First, who are you and how were you wounded? Then she would casually mention the silk scarf and note his reaction. She looked into the parlor and saw that the man was still sleeping; his mouth, slightly opened, emitted a soft snuffle. She tiptoed closer to inspect the linen cloth on his injured arm. It had light pink splotches, which appeared dried. His face looked relaxed, his mouth almost in a smile. Sarah prided herself on her ministrations and went around him to put more wood on the fire, now reduced to faintly glowing embers.

In the kitchen, she ate some of the manchet loaf covered with butter and mint and drank a weak wine, which she preferred over beer. She left the rest of the meal for Peter and the sleeping figure. Then she set about her chores. At midmorning she left the house to pick some apples from the orchard out back. The drenching rain of yesterday had stopped, but left puddles of water in many spots, which made walking difficult so she had to keep to the paths to avoid getting her boots covered with mud. She reached the orchard and began to pick some of the fruit that had fallen to the ground. *These bruised ones are perfectly suitable for pies and tarts,* she thought. From across the field, she heard Peter call out from the rear door.

"Miss Sarah, he's awake! Come quickly. He's trying to rise."

Sarah continued to pick until her basket was full and meandered her way back to the house. *It was a slim chance that he would be able to stand or even sit up,* she thought. To her surprise, the man was up, wrapped in a blanket, and demanding that Peter get his clothes. A little color had returned to his face as he leaned against the back of a chair to support himself. The expression on his face—one of arrogance and power—suggested strength and privilege. He had the look of a nobleman. When he saw Sarah, he stared at her so long that Sarah thought he had had a fit and was unable to move. Then she remembered her scar. He must be thinking how ugly it is.

"Whom do I have the pleasure of addressing?" she said, hoping to get his mind off her disfigurement.

"Madam, I am Robert of, of Salisbury," he stammered. "And you are…?"

It was Sarah's turn to stare at him. *If he is indeed from Salisbury,* she thought, *he might very well be connected to the Sidney family.*

"Madam, I told you my name. It is only proper that you tell me yours."

"My name is Sarah, and you need to sit in that chair before you fall over."

He smiled slightly at her command.

"Certainly, madam. Whatever you wish."

Sarah wasn't sure if he was being sarcastic or merely polite. He moved slowly to the front of the chair and sat down with a thump.

He was about to speak, but Sarah saw her opportunity and jumped in.

"Last night I removed a bullet from your arm. How did—"

"You removed the bullet? All by yourself?" He looked amazed.

"Yes, all by myself," Sarah said smugly, amused by his astonished expression.

"And did you undress me as well?"

"Peter helped me. Your clothes were soaked through, and your body felt icy cold. There was no other way to warm you up. Your garments are drying out back. I had to unlace some seams to get them off you, and I will bind them together when they are dry. Perhaps in a few hours."

"I see. I do not wish to remain undressed. Does your husband have breeches and a shirt I can wear?"

Sarah wondered if she should tell him the truth. Being alone in this house with a man could be dangerous, as she well knew. Maybe she could get away with a half-truth.

"I do not have a husband, but my father is expected back this morning."

"Your father? Then perhaps I might wear some of his clothes."

Sarah considered that possibility but realized that her father was not much taller than she was and very slim. This man, although slim, had the height of the king's bodyguards.

"There is nothing that would fit you, and since you are too weak to travel, you must wait until yours are dried and stitched. I will bring you a long linen shirt to cover yourself but first, tell me how you came to be wounded."

Robert hesitated. He had no idea where he was or what connections this woman's family might have with his enemies.

"It is a long story and—"

"Well, Robert, you are here for the day. I doubt you will need more time than that to explain," she cut in.

Robert could tell she was determined to get an answer. He needed time to think.

"Yes, of course I will tell you, but first, may I ask where I am?"

"You are at The Mews, property that has been in my family for generations."

"The Mews? What town is it near?"

Sarah smiled. "Nothing really. We are nearly a half morning's journey to Wells."

"Ah, I understand why The Mews was so named. A secret, hidden place."

"Only to those who are not from around here. And now for your long story."

"Perhaps I might have some food first, if your hospitality will extend that far?"

Sarah reddened. *How can I be so rude,* she thought, *to question this man before offering him sustenance.*

"Of course. I will bring you some manchet bread and beer."

When Sarah left the room, Robert considered his options. He could tell her about the battle with his family's enemies who were trying to take their land, or he could pretend he was hit by a hunter's stray bullet. Chances were good that in this remote region, she and her father were unaware of his family and their quarrel with Essex, but there was a cleverness about Sarah that made him think it was best to be open and honest with her.

When Sarah returned, she carried a long linen shirt along with a cloth to fashion a sling for his left arm and some bread and beer. He sipped the beer and broke off small pieces of the bread and chewed slowly, savoring the first meal he had had in almost a day. He had eaten bread served in a tenant's kitchen on his father's northernmost property and thought it tasteless. This, covered with butter and sage, was quite good. *There is nothing like a tasty meal to make one think clearly,* he thought. Robert swallowed the last morsel, licked his lips, and let out a sigh. Finally, he knew what he would tell this quick-witted woman whom he knew wanted answers to his present condition.

Sarah, watching him, thought at least he was a man who had been taught how to eat properly. She burned to know more about him. The man before her was a person of some consequence, to be sure.

When he finished his simple meal, he said, "That was very satisfying. And now for my long story. My family has some land near Salisbury, which is east of here."

"I know where Salisbury is," Sarah snapped.

"Oh! Do you, now? My family name is Dudley."

"I have heard of them." She shrugged and made it sound as though that noble family were nothing special but also thinking that it was possibly a lie.

"Really? And how it that so?"

Sarah ignored the question. "Your long story, please! About your wound. Remember?"

"Yes, yes. It is only you who can ask the questions. My family is in battle with Essex who is trying to take land that is in dispute. I was sent to discuss a settlement when two of Essex's men recognized me and told me to turn back. Naturally, I refused. I can easily beat two men with swords, but as we fought, two more men came carrying muskets and immediately started shooting at me. I nearly escaped without a scratch."

"Harrumph! Nearly but not completely. Why did you not tell the first men you saw of your intention?"

"You do not understand," he said. "They were just servants. They would not have believed or even comprehended my motives. They like to fight."

"And, apparently, so do you. But you, being wiser and more articulate, should have been able to convince them otherwise."

"Never!"

"Well, at least you could have tried. Disputes can last for generations, even centuries. Look at England and Spain, or Rome and—"

"Heavens!" he shouted. "How can you know all this?"

"I have read about it in books," she said matter-of-factly.

His eyes went all around the spartanly furnished room. "How can you afford books, and where did you learn to read? Who taught you to remove bullets from bodies, and how dare you question my actions?" he screamed.

So angry did Robert appear that for a split second, Sarah thought she was in the presence of the man who had attacked her fourteen years ago. She was not accustomed to such rage, never from her mild-mannered father or any other man she came in contact with. What kind of man was this who would scream at the person feeding and sheltering him? Silence filled the room, while Robert's words hung in the air like icicles waiting to dissolve or crash to the ground. Sarah realized that both of them had their blood up and further questioning about his silk scarf would be futile. He had taken great offense at her suggestion that he had acted beneath his rank, and she was put out by his assuming she was ignorant and disrespectful. She took a deep breath.

"Perhaps we should stop asking questions for a while. I have chores to do."

She turned on her heels and headed for the buttery, thinking what kind of a guest, and a gentleman at that, insults his host. His manners were abominable. She left the house through the rear passageway, angry with herself because she had not found out Robert's connection to the Sidney family.

Chapter Four

October 1607
The Mews
A Woman of Mystery

Robert stared after her. *How dare she turn and leave without me giving her permission,* he thought. *Who was she, anyway? Just a simple country woman living in rural England with not even a husband to teach her.* He had never questioned a woman's knowledge and abilities before, but almost all of the women he was acquainted with were titled. Most were taught embroidery and manners, how to play a musical instrument and parlor games. Perhaps they had a rudimentary knowledge about history and literature but certainly never challenged a man about his actions. And how did she learn so much? There was nothing in the parlor to indicate wealth or learning; it was just a large room with a fireplace in the center of one wall and a wooden chair on either side. He turned around and noticed a portrait of a man hanging on the opposite wall, probably an ancestor. In one corner was an oak cupboard and in the other a trestle table and a bench. This room was what he expected to see in a home in the rural countryside. He decided to look further. There was a door on the far side of the room, most likely a storage area. He unwrapped the blanket that was covering him and put on the long linen shirt and slipped the sling about his left arm. Then Robert walked slowly across the parlor and opened the door.

What he saw left him dumbfounded. It appeared to be a library with shelves on all four walls, crammed with books and manuscripts. A very long table stood in the middle with a bench on either side and several oak chairs were pushed into the corners. It looked like a school or meeting room. He picked out one book nearest to him. It was entitled *Orlando Furioso*. A book written in Italian. He glanced at another one. *The Chronicle of England, Scotland and Ireland*. Incredulous, he read more titles: *Metamorphoses* in Latin and Plutarch's *Lives of Noble Grecians and Romans*. These books were rare and costly. Commoners were lucky if they had a *Bible* in their home.

Robert tried to piece together what he was seeing. This certainly was not a grammar school; these books were far too advanced for farmers' children to study. No one but the nobility had this many books and certainly not an interest in so many different subjects. How could Sarah's father afford these? Why would he spend so much money on books when he clearly was not wealthy? And what was the need for so large a table as well as benches and chairs? Maybe it was a literary academy, like the one his cousin, the Countess of Pembroke, had established at Wilton House, but to what end. It didn't make sense to find a scholarly establishment in such a rustic setting. He had heard of secret societies, like the Rosicrucians, whose members purportedly possessed secret wisdom, or the School of Night, which practiced atheism. Perhaps he had fallen, literally, into a den of iniquity. There was much more to Sarah's existence than what he had assumed. This was a puzzle that needed answers. He decided to stay and wait for her father to return. All of a sudden, his legs felt weak. The chair in the parlor was too far away, so he stretched out on the oak bench and closed his eyes.

When Sarah returned to the house through the rear door, she put down her basket and peeped into the parlor only to find Robert not there. Where would he have gone in just a nightshirt? She moved toward the front door, but then noticed that the library door on the opposite side of the room was ajar. She entered and found him fast asleep on the bench, the linen nightshirt spilling down to the floor.

"Robert! Get up! Go into the parlor. This is not where you should sleep." She would show him that she was not cowered by his scoldings.

Robert awoke with a start and smiled.

"Sarah, this is much more comfortable than the parlor floor, but if you insist." He started to rise but leaned heavily against the table, feigning weakness.

"Do you need help?" She would call Peter to come to give him a hand. But Robert, assuming it was she who was willing to help him, said yes and immediately put his good arm around her waist.

"This is much better," whispered Robert in a conspiratorial manner. A shudder went through Sarah. Flashes of the past came to her mind. *Will he attack me like the other one did?* She tried to dismiss the thought. Peter was in the barn, and Jane was due back shortly. She could call out for help if need be, but his demeanor, although disarming, was not threatening. She felt safe, which surprised her. Together the two of them took slow steps to the large oak chair by the fireplace. As he sat down, Sarah thought how strange it was to see another man in her father's favorite chair, one that Doctor Burton had designed and built himself. Robert's voice brought her back to the present.

"Now that I have told you my story, I wonder if you would tell me yours."

"My story?"

"It is very unusual to see so many books and papers in such a modest dwelling as this. Is your father a scholar?"

A modest dwelling, thought Sarah. *It is one of the largest homes in the village.* Her temper, which had been on a low simmer, was now up again.

"My father is many things." She practically spat out the words. "He is a doctor, an inventor, a chemist, and, yes, a scholar." She paused after each occupation so that he might fully appreciate her father's abilities. Robert seemed not to notice her anger.

"Really?" His raised eyebrows said it all. *Now he was questioning her father's pursuits,* she thought. The arrogance of the man was too much.

"What is his name? Perhaps I have heard of him."

"He is Dr. John Burton," Sarah said proudly.

"I am only familiar with a Robert Burton, the writer."

"We are distant cousins."

"Ah, well, then. I am most anxious to meet your father. You said he was expected home today."

"Well, yes, but weather or business may delay him." She knew he would not be home until tomorrow, but her lie, once begun, had to continue.

Just then, Jane, a frail-looking girl with deep blue eyes and light brown hair, entered the room and immediately started upon seeing Robert. She wore a white cotton apron that went down to her ankles, clearly much too big for her short frame.

"Jane, thank goodness you have returned. How is your sister?"

"Much better, Miss Sarah." Jane's eyes stayed fixed on the stranger sitting in the parlor of her mistress's house wearing nothing but a nightshirt and a sling.

"This man is Robert of Salisbury. He was wounded in a-a skirmish and found his way to our door. He will be here until his clothes are dry and laced up. You may get on with your chores."

Turning to Robert, she said curtly, "You may sit there or lie down by the fire if you like. I will be outside in the garden. If you need anything, ask Jane to call for Peter, the stable boy."

"I have a purse in my saddlebags. Perhaps you could ask Peter to bring it to me. I must repay you for your kindness."

"That is not expected or wanted," she said frigidly. "We are hospitable to all strangers and do not accept payment from them."

Turning away, her face as red as her hair, she stormed out of the room.

Chapter Five

October 1607
The Mews
The Parting

The day passed without any further interaction between Sarah and her unwanted visitor. Jane gave Robert a lunch of meat, bread, and ale and began to re-lace his coat, which was now mostly dry. His leather breeches were still damp and hung on a hook by the fireplace. The silk scarf, washed and pressed, was returned to Robert who thanked Jane and tied it around his neck.

Without Sarah around, Robert felt safe to ask the girl more about the Burtons, but she was not very forthcoming. She had worked at the house for several years, having taken over when old Mrs. White passed on, and she was treated kindly and enjoyed her work. Often there was much activity. Local folks dropped in to be treated for various ailments or visitors who came from far away had to be fed and bedded. No one was ever refused entry.

"Visitors from far away?" asked Robert. "What is their purpose in coming here?"

"Well," Jane began, "I don't rightly know. That is, I never go into the library to listen to them talk. Sometimes it is so crowded in there, men must sit on the floor outside the door. They talk well into the night."

"Really? And these men all come from long distances, you say?"

"Oh, no, sir. Not all. There are local farmers and tradesmen as well. The shepherd talks quite a bit. He has a loud voice, and I can hear him from most anywhere in the house."

"The shepherd talks with the gentlemen?"

"Aye, sir. He certainly has his say on whatever is the matter." She brushed her hair away from her eyes and glanced toward the door into the buttery, anxious to get on with her chores.

"How often do these discussions take place?"

Jane paused, considering the question. Then, looking down at her scuffed boots, she said,

"Can't really say, sir." Jane raised her head and gave Robert a pleading look, twisting her fingers and moving her feet in the direction of the buttery.

Robert finally noticed her fidgetiness. He beckoned her closer and took her hand, and gave her a warm smile.

"Thank you, Jane. You have been most helpful. I shall look forward to meeting your master today."

"Today, sir? But Miss Sarah told me that the master is not expected until tomorrow. Gone to Wells on business with Jack, his servant."

"I must have misunderstood."

When Jane left, Robert sat back in the sturdy oak chair and reviewed what he had just learned. *Sarah lied to me,* he deduced, *but why?* He stared at the blazing fire, trying to connect the pieces of information he had gleaned from Jane. Ordinarily, farmers and tradesmen kept to themselves and never had any interaction with gentlemen unless for business. Maybe, Robert reasoned, these men are Catholics who are planning an insurrection to overthrow King James. In that case, it was his duty to report such meetings to the Crown. He decided to remain at the Mews to try to learn more.

Later in the day, with his jacket and breeches now dried and mended, Robert had little excuse for staying another night, but he thought of a way to remain without causing suspicion so he could investigate the mystery more thoroughly. He needed to get to the stable, so he opened the heavy oak front door and walked outside. The dirt road was just steps away. How could he have missed seeing this house when he first arrived? Looking up and down the path, he saw fields and trees extending as far as the eye could see. It was fortunate that his horse stopped where it did. There was no other house around. He turned around to take a good look at the dwelling. In front of him stood a sturdy, two-story edifice, timber-framed and white-washed with a sloping, thatched roof. It had two chimneys, one in the middle of the roof and the other on the far end. Apparently, the second chimney and the glazed windows were recent additions, which gave the whole structure a modern look. It was a comfortable-looking dwelling, but nothing remarkable, he thought. Just what he expected a respectable country doctor would have.

He moved slowly over to the stable in the rear to check on his horse. The animal looked in fine shape, but Robert pretended that it had picked up a stone and had a sore hoof. It needed another day or two to heal. Sarah was still incensed by Robert's doubting her extensive knowledge of medicine and history, so she had Jane prepare a supper of meat, bread, and ale for Robert, telling her that a simple meal was enough for such a haughty visitor. She went upstairs, feigning fatigue. She wanted nothing more to do with such a man.

Jane, however, had different ideas; she quite liked the handsome gentleman who treated her so kindly. Before she left to go home, she slipped him a large slice of pie. Robert's eyes lit up at the sight of it.

"Apple pie is my favorite," he whispered.

"Please don't tell Miss Sarah on me," she begged.

He reached into the lining of his coat and took out a gold sovereign, pressing it into Jane's hand. Jane's eyes lit up. "It will be our secret," he whispered, while putting his finger to his lips. He had decided that since Sarah would not accept any payment for her services that he would transfer his appreciation to her servant. He ate the pie in three swallows and decided it was definitely worth a gold coin.

That evening Robert did not go to bed right away. The information he had gleaned from Jane remained on his mind. What could explain late-night meetings with gentlemen and commoners? He remembered how upset Sarah was when she found him sleeping in the library. Now he went back in there to poke around some more.

The candlelight was so meager that he needed to keep the flaming wick close to his face to read the titles on the books. Most of the tomes were familiar to him; either he had read them or heard about them. But there was one well-thumbed study on *The Advancement of Learning,* only recently published by Francis Bacon that raised his suspicion. It discussed secret codes and ciphers, especially the number thirty-three and its prevalence in mathematical symbolism. Had he, Sir Robert Dudley, come across a member of a secret society that was outlawed by the Crown and the Church? And if he had, what was he to do about it? He left the library more confused than before.

The next day John Burton arrived home at mid-morning. When he entered his house, Sarah greeted him warmly and explained the circumstances of Robert's presence and then, excusing herself, left the house to gather up the last of autumn's harvest. Although slightly stooped-shouldered and white-haired, the doctor had the slender body and robust appearance of a man half his age. His soft voice and clear hazel eyes evoked a feeling of trust and caring. The doctor immediately relayed news of his own. He and his servant Jack had left Wells in the early morning and had come across some men from Salisbury looking for a Robert Dudley who they believed was injured in a fight. What a surprise to find Robert in his very house.

"Your family is quite concerned for you, Sir."

"I plan to return home soon. Your daughter has told me something of your accomplishments and your generosity. I am very pleased to make your acquaintance."

"And I, yours. It is an honor to have a Dudley in my humble house."

"I noticed you have a very extensive collection of books. How on earth did you come to own so many?"

A flash of surprise passed across Dr. Burton's eyes.

"So you have seen my library?"

"Yes, and I could not believe the variety and extent of your collection."

Robert noticed that Burton had not answered his question yet. He pressed on.

"Do you hold an academy here?"

"Yes. I suppose you could call it that. I try to educate and enlighten men of all backgrounds about the world."

"So Jane has said. Very unusual to say the least."

The doctor's brow became furrowed, and his eyes narrowed.

"When is your group assembling next? I would like to hear how the discussions tend."

The doctor stared long and hard at Robert, as if trying to read his mind. He stared so long that Robert became embarrassed and shifted his feet, causing the floor to creak.

Finally, John Burton said in a matter-of-fact tone, "They come this very night. If you wish to stay, you will meet some men with far greater accomplishments than my own. Some are learned, and some have a natural intelligence and sense about them. Our talks are never dull."

Robert considered his invitation. Apparently, there was nothing so radical as an insurrection happening here, but he was still curious to see a group of men from different professions and social standings discuss issues in an open and amiable way. He had never heard of such a thing.

"I am much obliged. I am most anxious to see how this collection of learned and self-taught men consider worldly matters. And I am most impressed by the number of books in your library."

"I procure some by bartering with wealthy or educated men I meet, and some of the manuscripts are copies. Come here and let me take a look at your wound." Robert obliged by removing his sling and rolling up his sleeve. The doctor searched in his pocket for his spectacles, and placed them on his nose with a great flourish.

"Without these, I can't tell a mouse from a musket ball." He turned Robert's left arm toward the window, then undid the binding and examined Sarah's work.

"Yes, it is healing nicely. I must tell Sarah that she is better at stitchery of this kind than I am." He smiled proudly and then said, in almost a whisper, "Her life is one of service to others. Commendable for sure but far different from what I imagined for her years ago. I raised her by myself, you see, after losing my wife in childbirth. I wanted to teach her everything I knew, thinking that she would marry a man who valued medical knowledge. She proved to be an excellent student and wanted to know more. She, being female, could not attend school so I brought home books and together we read and discussed their contents. Then I realized it would be beneficial to have men with differing views come here to argue over matters so she might know opposing views. Perhaps I went too far for now she revels in the give and take of ideas from the hodgepodge of men who attend these gatherings. In short, she has become so knowledgeable that she is unsuitable to marry any man who is not as learned as she is."

He stopped talking and shook his head, as if trying to erase the past from his mind. "And I also failed her in another way."

"How so?"

Dr. Burton turned his face away so Robert wouldn't see the tears welling up. "I don't suppose she told you how she got the scar on her face."

Robert heard the anguish in the doctor's voice and placed his right hand on Dr. Burton's arm. "No,", he said, his own voice barely a whisper.

"Just as well. It is an horrific story and one that I want to forget." He sighed deeply. "But I can't. If only I had been home…" His eyes glazed over, and his body trembled.

Robert thought better than to probe further. Whatever happened to Sarah was violent and most likely prevented her from marrying. His mind went through possible scenarios, each one more horrible than the other. He needed to change the subject.

"I have seen for myself how Sarah is quite good in rhetoric as well as stitchery. She countered my every utterance with a rebuttal that would have pleased Socrates."

Burton laughed so hard, his spectacles almost fell off. "Yes, yes. She can argue a dog off a bone. When she chooses to speak at a gathering, everyone pays attention to what she says. Her logic is well thought out. She has made many a visitor sound foolish. If she were a man, that might carry her far, but it is a gift that will remain hidden from most of the world."

"May I spend some time in your library? Your collection is most impressive, and I am sure that I will learn much from passing my time in such a manner."

The doctor gave his assent, and after taking a manuscript from his travel bag that he had obtained in Wells, headed for the library himself. The two men read silently on opposite sides of the table for most of the afternoon. A thought crossed Robert's mind that perhaps Dr. Burton wanted to keep an eye on him, but for what reason, he could not imagine.

That evening a dozen men gathered in John Burton's library, a few in finely woven silk coats and breeches but most in simple flannel or coarse linen garments. As Dr. Burton greeted each person, he pulled him close and whispered something in his ear, before introducing him to Robert. Robert noticed this and assumed that the doctor was simply explaining who Robert was. When Robert spoke to them, the men were polite but kept their comments general and vague. Obviously Burton knew these men intimately, so a nobleman in their midst must have been unusual. There was much banter among them; class differences did not seem to matter here. The first topic of the evening was about the use of the forest by nobles. Why did only they have the right to hunt there? Why couldn't commoners cut down trees for firewood? Were the fish in the sylvan streams within the forest the province of the nobility alone, and if not, how could a commoner catch them if he was not allowed to enter the woods? The men who owned land sided with the nobles' view that the king had the right to control the forests and the streams. The farmers, craftsmen, and laborers pressed for allowing some hunting, fishing, and logging to take place to ease the needs of the commoners.

Sarah, who had been listening in silence up to now, raised her head and in a soft voice, asked, "Does the king have the right to control everything within his realm?"

"Yes, of course," a plump squire answered, dismissive of the very question.

"Then I cannot take a breath without the king's permission?" Sarah queried.

"That is different," the same squire replied.

"How is it different?" countered Sarah.

Other, smarter men in the room who saw where this line of questioning was going, sat back and smiled. They knew this pompous squire didn't stand a chance to win this argument.

"Because everyone must breathe in order to live." The squire smirked at her and settled back in his chair.

"Yes, that is true," said Sarah. "And everyone must also eat in order to live. If the only food for the king's subjects is in the woods and the streams, then by denying access to them, the king is also denying his subjects the right to life, no?"

"Well, no, that's not exactly true. Poor men can eat nuts and berries—"

"Most of which are in the woods belonging to the king."

"What about fish from the sea?"

"Poor men do not have boats or nets, and many live miles away from any sea coast."

"Well, I am sure they make do. They always have."

"Then why are there so many dying and starving people in our country, if indeed, they are making do?" was Sarah's reply.

The squire could not deny that men, women, and children died of hunger every day. His face turned red with embarrassment. Finally he said, "You talk nonsense." Not a very good response; the squire as much as admitted defeat.

"Touche!" exclaimed another squire. "She bested you yet again." The other men around the table chuckled, while Robert laughed inwardly at how clever Sarah was at asking questions that, little by little, led to the outcome she had anticipated.

The subject was dropped, and the group moved on to other matters. As the evening wore on, the arguments became more heated but never violent. Each person was given the same opportunity and respect as another. Robert was at once impressed by the civility shown to others of whatever rank and, at the same time, unsettled by it. This was not the natural way English society behaved. He wondered if these men behaved this way toward other men when they walked the streets of their cities and towns. He decided to ask Dr. Burton later.

Sarah left the room about midnight, and the others began to leave in twos and threes. No one wanted to travel home alone at night because of the possibility of being attacked by highwaymen. Two of the gentlemen were to spend the night at the Mews, along with Robert.

The next morning broke partly cloudy and cool, a good day for travel. There was no opportunity to talk to the doctor alone, so Robert just thanked him once again and looked about for Sarah.

"Dr. Burton, where is your daughter? I wish to speak with her before I leave."

"I believe she is out in the garden, picking up the leavings from the harvest. We try to find a use for everything Nature gives us."

He gave Robert a questioning look. "She seems somewhat put out with you. She told me this morning that you questioned her medical training and her knowledge of history. She takes great offense when her abilities are doubted."

"But…I didn't mean. I-I had no idea—"

Robert felt like he had been punched in the stomach. His visceral reaction startled him. He wanted her good will, but he didn't understand why that was important to him. He had been impressed by Sarah's logic during the discussion with the squire and how her responses had boxed in his arguments until he had no answer but to dismiss her. There was only one woman he had ever met or even heard of who could compare with her for reasoning abilities as well as medical knowledge, and that was his cousin Lady Anne Herbert whose entire family revered literature, science, languages, and history. Lady Anne had been expertly tutored; Sarah, however, had only read books acquired by her father. It seemed *impossible that both women had similar knowledge and rhetoric. In one* day Sarah had gone from being a somewhat clever woman to one with formidable command of thought and language. He needed to find her and explain himself. That he had known her only two days did not matter.

He quickly left the house and entered the expansive garden. There were long rows of plant stalks, now mostly stubs. These rows extended all the way to an orchard; the fields on either side of the garden ended at the woods. He did not see her anywhere. Perhaps she had gone back in the house by the front entrance. He was about to turn around when she appeared at the edge of the far wood, with a basket in her hand. As he moved toward her, she suddenly turned and disappeared among the trees. *She must have seen me and wants to avoid a meeting*, he thought. *Well, I am not leaving without apologizing.* He caught up to her in a vale. She looked surprised to see him.

"I am searching for some mushrooms," she said curtly, brushing away some leaves from the hem of her white petticoat. Being alone with a man in a wood made her uneasy. She knew it was not proper. How was she supposed to act in front of a tall, handsome nobleman who found her there? She turned away from him and bent to pick up a white capped beauty, brushing away the dirt and placing it in her half-filled basket.

"Sarah, I am leaving and I want to apologize to you before I go. I am sorry if I offended you." He could hardly believe he was saying this. Robert had never apologized to a woman for anything, not even to his mother when he was a naughty boy. Sarah did not respond, so he continued. "I am in awe of your abilities. You are a most competent woman."

Now she turned and stared at him. Was he serious? Did he, a titled man, really believe that she was smart and clever? Now that she understood him to be a nobleman, she was ashamed of how forcefully she had questioned his behavior toward his enemies. His eyes and expression showed an earnestness that appeared heartfelt. She kept looking at him, expecting to see a smirk that showed he was joking. To Robert, her lips looked warm and inviting. Robert had a sudden urge to kiss her.

The sky, which had been mostly a thin blanket of gray, suddenly cleared, and a burst of sunlight fell through the trees at an angle, covering Sarah's body like a flaming torch, illuminating the space around her. The light made her eyes dazzle with gold-green hues, and her red hair appeared to sparkle like jewels in a tiara. It was too much for him to resist.

"Please forgive me," he begged. Her mouth opened slightly and without waiting for her to answer, he bent over and kissed her with lips so hot, that she felt her lips had become inflamed. With great effort, Sarah pulled away, flushed and bewildered by his action and her reaction.

"Please, please forgive me," he whispered, taking her hand in his and kissing her again with more passion. Sarah felt his body against hers and tasted the pleasant sage from his breakfast still on his lips. She could feel his heart pounding or was it her heart; she could not tell which was which.

It didn't matter. Neither of them drew back this time. The squawk of a crow close by gave alarm that made Sarah finally retreat. Her legs could no longer support her and she swayed, putting her arms out for balance, almost tipping her basket. Robert held onto her hand to steady her. She reached out for something to support her and found his sling and immediately moved her hand away, not wanting to hurt his wounded arm. Her hand came to rest on his chest, and she did not want to take it away. They remained for some moments, looking into each other's eyes without speaking. Then they heard voices in the distance and, embarrassed, moved away from each other.

"Are you all right?" he said softly.

"Yes." Her voice was barely audible.

The moment of passion had passed, and they walked back to the manse together, each deep in thought. The recent rain had steeped the garden in earthy smells, with swirls of luxuriant chocolate and coffee-colored soil. As their feet pressed into the wet earth, they made a sucking sound, sensuous and pleasing. By the time they reached the front walk, their emotions were at a full gallop. Peter had Robert's horse saddled and held it for him. Robert reached into his saddlebag, took out his purse, and handed Peter a gold sovereign, thanking him for the care of his horse. Peter stared at the coin in disbelief.

"But this is a gold coin, Sir," Peter said, thinking Robert had made a mistake. Robert shook his head and smiled. "It's yours, Peter. Spend it wisely." The taste of Sarah's kiss was still on his lips, and he was feeling generous. There was nothing left for Robert to do but gingerly grab the reins with his left hand and, holding on to the saddle horn with the other, swing his right leg over to mount his horse. He turned to Sarah to bid her farewell, but she was already heading into the house.

Chapter Six

October 1607
Salisbury
Elizabeth's Judgment

The road back to Salisbury was filled with tradesmen; some were trudging along the muddy, bumpy road, laden down with cloth, wax candles, knives and other household wares, while farmers rode on wagons full of late season crops to be sold in the marketplace. Peasant women with baskets in one hand and a child in the other, scurried behind the wagons, hoping for some edible morsel to fall out and land at their feet. Travel on market day was slow going for anyone but the queen, whose guards could force everyone off the highway to make way for her majesty's majestic entourage.

Robert barely noticed the congestion; his mind swirled with thoughts of Sarah, their kiss, and of her father's academy. It was all so extraordinary to him that he felt he had been dreaming. To find a house in the countryside with so many books and to listen to such an odd mixture of men, along with Sarah, debate political matters both amazed and frightened him. It was against the way things had existed for centuries, he reasoned. King James was not partial to yeomen and craftsmen rising above their station, so if John Burton was found out, he would be imprisoned. It was just the information that his older brother Edward kept his ears alert for in his efforts to please the king and gain more titles. Edward's zeal to become a member of the king's inner circle sometimes worried Robert because his brother had bragged at how he had beaten suspected traitors before dragging them into London for questioning. Edward had convinced the Crown of plots that were, at best, no more than grumblings. What would he have made of last night's meeting? The men in Burton's library were defying convention, but was what they were discussing really treasonous? Robert knew that he should inform the monarchy; however, he did not feel that what the doctor was doing was dangerous to the Crown, though a local spy might and report them to the king. In that event, the Burtons' lives were endangered. He became distraught at the thought of Sarah and her father being carted off to jail or even beheaded for acting in an improper manner. No, it could never happen; the king had more important matters to occupy his time.

He began to replay the kiss in his mind, how he pressed his lips to hers, and how Sarah reacted to it. Her kiss was so sweet, so, so accepting. Even Anne's kisses did not burn as hot as hers. Her lips had tasted like mint and the glow in her eyes spoke to him of desire. *I wonder if Sarah is thinking about me,* he mused. A deep sigh escaped his lips. He was beginning to miss her already.

But as he got closer to home, his thinking changed and he chided himself for kissing a woman he barely knew. He had let his emotions rule his judgment. Sarah was a commoner, for mercy sake, but then again, not at all common. The kiss, brief as it was, filled him with longing. Was it because of the loss of Anne soon after their engagement or the absence of any woman, he was not sure, but he was overcome with an acute loneliness. *This is a temporary attraction,* he reasoned. *I will get over it once I am home. I must push all thoughts of her out of my mind.*

When Robert reached the bustling town of Salisbury, he met up with a retinue of his father's servants who insisted on escorting him to Tisbury

Manor. A report that he had been shot during an altercation had reached his parents, and search parties had been scouring the countryside looking for him. After giving his father a sketchy report on his meanderings, he went to look for his sister, Elizabeth. He found her in a parlor chair, her tall frame leaning against a bolster as she read a book of poetry, while her maids embroidered cushions.

"Hello, Sister! I see you are improving your mind rather than your handiwork."

Her dark brown eyes lit up, and she twisted her head around when she heard his voice.

"Robert! You have come back in one piece. Did you behave bravely and honorably as Father expects you to do?"

"Of course, although I may have left a little piece of my left arm in a small village near Wells. Listen to what I found there."

"I am all ears."

Robert expounded on his adventures to his sister, about his arrival at the Mews, his being expertly doctored by a woman and her vast knowledge of medicine, history, and philosophy. He described how during a meeting, she argued with a man of high rank and stood her ground until he had no rebuttal against her views. When he finally finished, he saw that Elizabeth was smiling broadly.

"What amuses you so much?"

"You, Brother. I have never seen you this animated in many a month. You are in love with this Sarah woman, aren't you?"

"No, no. Of course not. She is a commoner. But it does make me wonder what she would be if she were a man and of noble birth."

"A king, no doubt, from your description of her knowledge and power over people. I must meet her to see if everything you say about her is true.

Why don't you invite her to visit us in two weeks when we have some noted people arriving? Cousin Mary Sidney and Sir Francis Bacon will be here and Dr. John Dee as well. They are all lovers of history and the sciences. If Sarah is as clever as you purport, there is bound to be some captivating discussion."

"She is a commoner; they would be appalled to have such a person as part of their discourse."

"Are you afraid she may prove to be unskilled in those areas?"

Robert knew his sister was baiting him, but the prospect of seeing Sarah again and the idea of showing her his family's estate began to please him, and because Sarah and her father had deep knowledge, he doubted that they would embarrass themselves by speaking in front of such a learned gathering.

"Yes, I will invite her. And her father as well. I want to repay them for their hospitality toward me." He left the parlor in great haste, bumping into a table.

Elizabeth laughed so hard the auburn ringlets around her head bounded up and down. She sat back on her rose-colored cushions in deep satisfaction. Her brother was finally out of his mourning for Anne, a cousin to whom Elizabeth had been very much attached. She wished that Robert and Anne had been allowed to wed, for their dispositions mirrored each other's closely. They both enjoyed music, dancing, hunting, and discussing historical and political matters. Being third cousins made such a marriage politically pleasing to both families, but it was not enough to sway King James.

Several things about Anne's death still puzzled Elizabeth. She was reported to be sickly, but she never appeared wan or weak. Her death in Cambridge came as a shock to her closest friends, even though she had stayed away from Court from time to time because of ill health. And what was more perplexing was why didn't Cousin Mary bring Anne's body back to Salisbury and bury her in the family tomb in the cathedral? When she herself went to Cambridge to pray at Anne's grave, she could not find it.

Chapter Seven

November 1607
The Mews
The Invitation

After Robert left the Mews, Sarah kept busy with preserving herbs and mending some garments. She had tried to read but could not keep her mind on the passages. She kept asking herself, *Why did I allow him to kiss me? I should have slapped his face.* Then she thought about how surprised and pleased she felt afterwards. He wanted to kiss her; she had enjoyed it as well. That night she tossed and turned in bed with thoughts that she had never had, with sensual feelings that bubbled up inside. *This is madness,* she mused. *I must be rational. I am never going to see him again, so why do I even think about any meaning behind the kiss?* Finally she fell asleep with the conviction that since it was likely to be the only passionate kiss she would ever get and since she would certainly never see him again, her behavior was acceptable.

A few days later, a rider came galloping up to the house with a letter for her father. The doctor read it and chuckled.

"It is from Robert, Sarah. He wants us to visit him at his estate in Salisbury on Saturday next. He is having some guests that he would like us to meet. Dr. John Dee, Sir Francis Bacon, and his cousin Lady Mary Sidney among others. Did he tell you that he was a cousin of the late Sir

Robert Dudley, who was a close confidante of Queen Elizabeth? What an honor to be asked to the estate of such a nobleman."

Sarah was astonished. *He must have met the king himself,* she thought. Despite her attempt not to blush, she felt her face burn and her heart throb with longing to see him again. She tried to think clearly. Why was Robert doing this, inviting her and her father to his estate? To repay them for helping him when he appeared at their door? There was no need to invite them to his home. That was not expected. And she knew so little about him. He was indeed related to the Sidneys who were also a titled, wealthy, and learned family. That alone would make him very desirable as a husband. Why was he not married? Or maybe he was! That notion startled and upset her. Maybe he was the type of man to kiss a woman he hardly knew even if he was already wed. He wore no wedding ring, but many men preferred not to wear one. He said he was on an errand of peace when he was set upon by men employed by Essex. Why did they assault him so violently? So many questions that begged for answers.

Her father's voice broke through her thoughts. "We will be guests in a great manor house. Robert Dudley must feel deeply obligated to repay our hospitality; most nobility would simply offer to repay a kindness with money or not at all." Sarah knew Robert had offered her money and she had refused. By doing so, she and her father were now going to meet his family. If nothing else, she hoped to get some further knowledge of Robert's past.

A thought suddenly struck her, causing her to shudder. What if the man who attacked her was invited to Robert's house as well? Her father had told her that her attacker must have been a nobleman for they are the ones who have the authority to root out enemies of the Crown. He explained that the nobility are a tight circle who eat, drink, and make merry with each other, even wedding their cousins to keep their property and titles within the family. She felt the pain again, the pain of a knife slashing at her. The image of the assailant flashed in her mind. His angry eyes, dark and steely, his youthful beard that had spit dribbling off it as he screamed at her, his words emanating from deep in his throat, the long iron dagger as it cut into her cheek; this kaleidoscope of images and sounds never went away. Most of all, she remembered the necklace, dangling from his neck as he bent over her. The chain was gold and had black onyx gems embedded in it, each one encased in a gold filigree. A thing of such beauty hanging from the neck of someone so evil.

She turned to face her father and was about to say that she did not want to go, that she would feel out of place in such an elegant manor, that she had no proper clothes for the occasion, but one glance at her father's smiling face stopped her. She had never seen him so happy. Ever since the attack on her nearly fourteen years ago, he had carried his guilt at not being home in his heart like a tortoise carries a shell—impossible to remove and so heavy to drag around.

"We will be dining, and conversing with highly educated people who have traveled widely and have written books on poetry, philosophy, science, and religion. This is more than I could ever have hoped for," the doctor chortled. "Sarah, you acted so bravely and wisely when you found Robert Dudley by our door. It is you I must thank for this invitation." He embraced her lovingly while chattering on about the visit to come. She hugged him back, but inwardly she trembled as she thought of how her common clothes, her country manners, and her scarred cheek would appear to wealthy and noble guests.

Chapter Eight

November 1607
Salisbury
The Welcome

Saturday, the day of their departure, came. Dressed in a green woolen skirt over a white petticoat and a pale green gown over that, Sarah knew she was not the height of fashion but she hoped to prove acceptable to the company she was to meet. She had packed her best outfits, and she chided herself on her conceit. *As if I could compete with rich, titled women,* she thought. *What am I trying to show? Not wealth, not fashion. Just good breeding, I guess.*

Sarah and her father, along with Jane, climbed into their new four-wheeled coach, a simple yet extravagant purchase her father had made months ago when his need for comfort triumphed over cost. To have an enclosed vehicle meant protection from rain, wind, and foul smells as well as a seat on which one could lean back and rest. Traveling on horseback was fine for young men who wanted speed for protection against highwaymen, but her father was now in his sixtieth year and troubled with arthritis.

During the ride, John Burton read through some recent correspondence whenever the coach found smooth roads; otherwise he closed his eyes as if deep in thought, mentally preparing for what was ahead. Sarah tried to prepare herself as well. If she was invited to join in discussions on the issues of the day, she promised herself to keep her comments vague. She did not want to call attention to herself or her father by questioning men of learning and stature; she was a guest at Robert's estate so she needed to hold her tongue.

As the coach entered Salisbury, Sarah's senses were assailed by the sights, sounds, and smells of market day. There was a myriad of stalls selling wool, cloth, vegetables, bread, and cheese as well as animals of every breed and size. The stench coming from their pens were particularly noxious, intermingling and becoming a pungent odor that permeated everything and everyone. It was both exciting and repugnant to her. Compared to her quiet hamlet, Salisbury burst with activity. The shopkeepers were obviously more industrious and wealthy, but the streets were filled with many poor and underfed residents. Disease-laden beggars were everywhere. In the town of Wells, everyone was known and looked after to some degree, but here it seemed an impossible task. Sarah did not envy the lord who had the responsibility of overseeing this incompatible mass of humanity.

Once through the city, the coach climbed up a long drive lined with tall pines and beyond those, fields of dried rapeseed, now having lost their yellow bloom. In the distance, Sarah saw the outline of a very large building. A cold shiver passed through her. Why had she ever agreed to come? Her heart beat so wildly that she felt it might explode. Her breathing became shallow. She prayed that Robert and his family would ignore her and focus only on her father.

The coach stopped in front of a majestic, two-storied gray stone building with four rows of double-hung windows on each side of the main entrance. Friezes and gargoyles decorated the roofline. *There must be dozens and dozens of rooms in this house,* Sarah thought. On each side of the building were gardens and paths. Across from the main entrance was a large lawn that ended at a pond inhabited by swans and egrets. She blinked her eyes, scarcely believing the idyllic scene before her. Suddenly, a shadow appeared at the coach door and a smiling face looked in. It was Robert, handsomely dressed in a doublet of red velvet, a silk waistcoat, and gray satin breeches. A footman opened the door, and Sarah descended on shaky legs. She curtsied to Robert, as she was expected to do for any titled person. Now she understood Robert's arrogant response to her questioning his behavior during their discussion of his skirmish with the men of Lord Essex. She was merely a commoner and, as such, had to show proper respect to those highborn.

Robert greeted her and her father warmly, but he appeared nervous. Sarah wondered if he had regrets about inviting commoners into his father's manor. As they turned to go up the steps into the building, a stunningly beautiful woman appeared at the door, dressed in a dark blue fitted jacket, a long blue skirt, topped with a matching brimmed hat and carrying a riding whip. Her dark hair and eyes matched Robert's, but the expression on her face was much brighter than his. She glided toward them as if on a moving carpet, exuding grace and elegance in every step. She had all the confidence of a woman who knew she could make people stop and stare just by being there.

"Ah," said Robert. "There is Elizabeth. She has been most anxious to meet you."

Sarah groaned inside. *Now I am to meet his wife. Why did I come?* she thought. *I do not want to be compared in beauty and style to such an elegant female.* She thought of her scar and suppressed an urge to hide it with her gloved hand. As Sarah climbed the stairs, she felt flushed and she knew that would only make the gash on her face more visible. When she got to the top step, she was surprised when Elizabeth kissed her warmly.

"I have heard so much about you from Robert. Since his return, he has talked of nothing else but his stay at your home."

Sarah looked surprised. "Really? I hope he found our accommodations adequate."

"He has never been so effusive in his compliments. My brother admires you greatly."

Sarah suddenly realized that Elizabeth was not Robert's wife, but his sister. She was so relieved that she felt light-headed and almost toppled backwards down the stairs. She jerked forward and steadied herself on the walk in front of the manor door.

"Thank you. I hope I can measure up," she said weakly.

The party entered the house and stopped in the great hall where Robert's parents were waiting. The high ceilings, gilded cornices, and marble floors with inlaid designs made both the Burtons feel not only humble but shabby. This was the grand manor of a noble family who claimed kinship with the king of England and to whom its occupants had now graciously granted admittance to two obscure country folk.

Lord and Lady Dudley stood like sentinels at the entrance to a castle. The wigged estate owner, portly and red-faced, typical of an aging nobleman whose entire life was blessed with abundance and pleasure, looked pained. *Perhaps his feet hurt from gout,* thought Sarah. *I should tell Father to mention the new treatment he recently heard about.* His lordship was smartly dressed in a handsome doublet and waistcoat of purple velvet and a linen shirt with a ruff around the collar. His thick legs were covered in satin stockings, and on his feet were smooth brown leather shoes. Lady Dudley, noticeably younger in age but just as plump, was dressed in a green silk gown with an embroidered kirtle over it that went from her collar to her ankles. Her petticoats hidden underneath were so wide that she took up three times the space as her husband did. Now she glared at Sarah and Dr. Burton with sullen eyes and a mouth so straight that it appeared she had no lips. Her eyebrows went at sharp angles from above her nose to her forehead, and stayed there. One would think they were entertaining the men who shot at their son, thought Sarah. The inconvenience of having to welcome the Burtons was clear, but Robert's parents did go through the motions of thanking the Burtons for tending to their son's wound. Their stiff bearing and clipped speech were in stark contrast to Robert and his sister Elizabeth's warm and welcoming demeanor. Sarah thought how strange it was to have parents and children so opposite in how they viewed themselves and how they behaved toward commoners.

Blessedly, the party moved on down the grand hall. Sarah and her father were escorted to a south-facing sitting room with windows that stretched from high up the walls to below a person's waist. There were so many windows bringing in so much light that Sarah was temporarily blinded from the brightness; it was just like being outside. The two windowless walls were covered with classical paintings encased in large golden frames, and much elaborate woodwork enclosed the fireplace, and squared off the ceiling and framed each window. Walnut chairs and sofas with delicately carved arms and legs were arranged in a circle in the middle of the room. Off to one side was an inlaid table which held decanters of French wine and trays of British scones. After they were all seated, a butler appeared and served each person with such a great flourish that Sarah felt like laughing out loud. *What silliness just to serve food and drink,* she thought. The pomp and ceremony made Sarah want to vaporize and reappear in the parlor of her home, surrounded by the heavy plain oak furniture she had known all her life. She slunk back in an enormous chair covered with red velvet and tried to make herself invisible. It did not work. In a short while, Elizabeth approached and asked if she would join her in a horseback ride around the estate. She assured Sarah that they would not be missed; Robert had to remain there for he was expected to stay with Dr. Burton, his invited guest. Lord and Lady Dudley were listening attentively while Dr. Burton was indeed explaining a new treatment for gout, ever prevalent among the gourmands who, as her father had observed during his travels, stuffed themselves with multiple courses, each containing four or five meat and fish dishes cooked with jellies or sauces. Her father was pleased to share his medical knowledge; Sarah was pleased to escape, but, although she was an accomplished rider, she was tired and had brought no appropriate attire.

"My clothes are not suited for such an exercise."

"That is quite all right," said Elizabeth. "You can borrow one of my outfits. We are about the same size."

Exhausted as she was, Sarah felt she should go. Robert's sister had paid her a great compliment by inviting her to ride, and Sarah wanted to show her appreciation. Robert watched the two ladies depart and wished he could join them, but he had to stay with Dr. Burton. Lord Dudley had been vehemently opposed to his son including these country people to so distinguished a gathering, saying, "They will embarrass us and insult our other guests," but Robert prevailed. He embellished his injury, called his loss of blood from his wound nearly fatal, saying he was delirious for a whole day before his condition improved, emphasizing how he was saved only by the hands of a competent woman and her father. His father finally relented on one condition. "They are your guests, so you must attend to their needs."

Once Sarah had changed her clothes, the ladies left the house by a side door, which led to the massive stables and storage sheds. Two horses were saddled and mounted. They proceeded along a dirt walk and soon reached waterfalls that cascaded down to ponds. Italian-style gardens were meticulously laid out with geometrical paths, and statues lined hidden sanctuaries. Never had Sarah imagined anyone living in such splendor. Elizabeth did most of the talking, pointing out certain late-blooming flowers and sharing her favorite spots to sit and read.

On their way back to the house, Elizabeth talked about Robert's life. Robert's elder brother, Edward, was to inherit the estate. As the second son, less was expected of Robert in terms of duty and marriage. He had been unlucky in his choices of brides. His first engagement, which was not his choice at all, was to a very young noble lady that Queen Elizabeth had decided was a fitting match. Robert thought she was plain looking and dull. The lady became sickly and was bedridden for so long that the wedding plans were abandoned. Then Robert became enamored by a distant cousin, Anne Herbert, who was the daughter of the Countess of Pembroke. Anne was equally enchanted, but the new monarch, King James, had decided that a recently widowed nobleman, the Earl of Hertford who was three times her age, was a better match for Anne. Robert and Anne were heartbroken, but hoped they could change the king's mind. For months they tried, but it proved impossible. Just before the expected engagement with the elderly widower, Anne abruptly left for Cambridge and shortly thereafter contracted an illness and died. It was she who had presented Robert with the silk scarf as a token of her love. Her body was never returned to her home, and when he looked for her tomb in Cambridge, he never found it. Robert was devastated. He had no outlet for his grief. His response was to engage in mock swordplay with his father's servants or go off on long, solitary rides around the estate. He ate poorly and grew a beard. His best friends became strangers to him. He never mentioned Anne again.

As Sarah listened to this account, she thought back to the night he appeared on her doorstep. He did indeed look like a recluse. Her heart was filled with pity that such a handsome, intelligent man should turn away from the world.

Chapter Nine

November 1607

Tisbury Manor

From Ecstasy ...

Robert was waiting for them.

"What took you so long? It's been hours since you left. I want to show Sarah the rest of the house before dinner."

"Calm down, Brother. There is plenty of time for that," said his sister as she dismounted from her mare. "She wants to see the stables first."

Sarah had not asked to see them but had no objection at all.

"Where is my father?" she asked.

"He has gone to his chamber to rest. You shall see him again at dinner." Robert helped her down from her horse and gave the reins to a groom. "I hope you were pleased with our gardens and woods."

"They are delightful. I would think you would never want to leave here."

"I am a second son, so this entire property goes to my brother Edward when my father dies. Such is the law of succession."

"Oh, yes. I am sorry. I forgot."

"No matter."

That evening, at an elaborate dinner, Robert had the chance to prove to Sarah that he was as good a host as she had been a hostess. His spirits were high; he fully expected that Sarah, in both looks and intelligence, would dazzle the other guests. He had insisted that Sarah be seated between him and Elizabeth. When he saw the two ladies enter the banquet hall, he beamed with pride. They were magnificently gowned in contrasting colors, Elizabeth in garnet red and Sarah in navy blue, a dress she had borrowed from her new friend. Sarah's hair was piled on top of her head and held in place with an ivory comb.

"Ladies, you light up this room with your beauty." Then he bent close to Sarah and whispered, "You are so lovely to look at that you take my breath away. I can hardly speak."

Sarah was taken aback. No one had ever told her that she was lovely to look at. Her father had always complimented her on her manners or her wit, but never on her looks.

"Thank you. Elizabeth came to my room with this silk gown and velvet slippers and hairpiece. She is so thoughtful and generous to me, I know not why."

"I taught her to be that way. The credit is all mine," Robert joked.

"How is your wound, Lord Robert?" Sarah asked, thinking how funny it sounded to call him by his proper title.

Robert gave a short laugh and whispered, "No need to call me Lord Robert unless I can call you Lady Sarah."

Sarah burst out laughing at the thought.

"I would be an imposter, but, if you insist, then I must imitate the behavior of a proper noblewoman," and she flattened her lips and frowned the way she had seen his mother do when she met her. Robert threw his head backed and roared. Then he wagged his finger at her in mock disapproval.

Elizabeth joined in the banter. "Perhaps Sarah would prefer to be called Doctor Burton. She cannot object to that title for she has certainly earned it."

"Ah," replied Sarah, wistfully, "that is an impossible reach for a backward country bumpkin like myself."

More laughter and banter followed. The happy trio were beginning to be noticed by the other guests at the table. Sarah saw Robert's father turn and glare at her. His eyes flashed with disapproval. *He should be happy that his one-time moody son is enjoying himself,* she thought. *Perhaps it's me he disapproves of. What do I care about what Lord Dudley thinks of me?*

She took another sip of the exquisite French wine and moved her head close to Robert's to listen to him carry on about how much he had enjoyed being cared for by a woman with extensive medical knowledge. *He's certainly changed his tune about me,* she thought. She found herself basking in Robert's and Elizabeth's company and relishing a dinner with course after course of meats, fish, cheeses, fruits, and rich desserts. It was such fun to converse with him and Elizabeth about the life of the upper class. The three of them whispered clever observations about the other guests and jests about how depopulated the forests must have become to fill this table with game, nuts, and berries. Sarah quite forgot her own comments made to the squire a fortnight ago about the starving population needing such food provided by the forests.

The others at the table were in a heated discussion about whether or not there was a need for magic in religion. It struck Sarah that magic, like exorcism and conjuring up spirits, was desired by the Church as a way to amaze the illiterate population and to keep the faithful in line, but she held her tongue. She had no desire to express her opinions among such elite company. A few at the table, like Francis Bacon and Lady Mary, were presenting opposing views. Dr. Dee kept insisting that he had made angels appear before him while in an altered state of consciousness. Sarah imagined that the famous doctor, now without his benefactor, Queen Elizabeth, needed his ego to be stroked.

In the meantime, Robert and Elizabeth were arguing over whose latest retort had been more clever. Sarah sat back and watched the siblings with envy. How she wished she had someone to share her joys and her hardships with. She realized that at twenty-eight, she did not have one person up to now, whom she could call a close friend. *So this is what having a sibling is like,* she thought. She wanted the bond she was creating with this brother and sister to continue. Having had a taste of upper class life, she no longer wanted to go back to the drab surroundings that had once satisfied her. *In any case,* she thought, *I will remember this night for the rest of my life. I am in ecstasy.*

Chapter Ten

November 1607

Tisbury Manor

...To Agony

After dinner they all proceeded to the grand parlor of Lord Dudley's house. This room was at least three times the size of the dining room and three times as intimidating. The dozen or so guests lined the room, seated in clusters, each with a glass of strong wine, presumably to help clarify their thinking.

Sarah now had a chance to observe the privileged class more closely. Robert's relative, Mary Sidney Herbert, was introduced as the Countess of Pembroke, his third cousin and mother of Lady Anne Herbert and a sixth cousin of the late queen. In her mind, Sarah could see the physical resemblance between the queen and Mary; both had curly red hair, blue eyes, aquiline noses, and oval faces. Mary's bright eyes and pleasing smile made her a most attractive lady. Known for her grace, wit, and intellect, as well as her piety, Mary was admired for her wide range of interests in many fields: poetry, literature, music, and science. Tonight she spoke about her interest in alchemy, noting how she and her assistant kept meticulous records of each formula they had tried.

"Yes. That is exactly right. That is what you must do in order to reach your objective. I believe that science and mathematical principles control our world," stated Sir Francis Bacon. As he spoke, his dark eyes studied the other guests as if attempting to read their minds. Bacon, at fifty-six years of age, had an impressive background, Elizabeth explained. He had been born into a wealthy family and thus was able to attend college where he studied science as well as law. He talked easily and knowingly on any subject under discussion. His essays on inductive reasoning and his treatise on scientific principles gave him unparalleled status among his fellow guests who hung on his every word.

He affirmed Lady Mary's use of record keeping and how what he called the scientific method would eventually lead to discoveries of all the mysteries on Earth and in the heavens.

"I even use mathematics in poetry," declared Lady Mary. "It was my brother Philip who invented the sonnet form that relies heavily on mathematics for its beauty. There are fourteen lines of verse, and each line has ten syllables, and each syllable has an unstressed and a stressed sound. When words are combined in such an orderly fashion, it is beautiful to hear."

"Indeed," agreed Sir Francis. "Mathematics is everywhere you look in the world."

"And in the heavens, too," rasped Dr. Dee. "I have studied the stars and have found that the laws that apply to earthly things are also true in the heavens. Let me explain where my investigations have led," and he droned on and on about his discoveries. Dr. John Dee, astrologer, magician, and mathematician, was the honored guest. He wore a black skull cap over his long white hair which seemed to flow into his very long beard and then down into his lap. To Sarah, he looked older than his eighty years, more like an ancient Greek philosopher who had been resurrected from the grave or like Death itself, complete with long, bony fingers and hawk nose. He had been an adviser to Queen Elizabeth, using his reputation as an astrologer to inform her of the best time to be crowned and when to go to war with Spain. Now, according to Robert's sister, he was depending on his past accomplishments to be still taken seriously. He spoke at length about his attempts to communicate with the spirit world, first by fasting and then by taking certain drugs that would put him in an altered state and how at times he had been successful.

As he spoke, Sarah noted that the other guests were receiving his claims with skepticism. Her father, in spite of being a commoner, had been allowed to sit in the midst of the distinguished group, and was staring at Dee with a look of disbelief. Sarah and Elizabeth were given chairs against the wall and tried to follow the discussion as best they could.

Later in the evening the talk turned to interest in the occult. What is the line between religious rituals and witchcraft? Did fairies truly exist? *Elizabeth and Sarah listened in rapt attention as the men displayed their* rhetorical skills. As the evening was coming to a close, with the port and brandy bottles nearly empty, the arguments grew more hazy and fragmented. Someone asked Dr. Dee if he believed in free will.

Dee replied, "There is no free will. There is only the divine plan. Everything happens according to God's law." His grayish black lips moved ever so slightly, as if the words were emanating from some magical place. "There is no such thing as chance. The rich and the poor live their lives according to the will of God."

There was silence while the assembly waited for someone to take an opposing view. Sarah saw several of the company nodding in agreement. Everyone appeared in favor of that belief. *How could no one object or at least give an opposing argument?* she thought. *Such a belief cannot go unchallenged.*

Finally, Sarah heard someone say, "Dr. Dee, don't we all choose our beliefs, our friends, our moods, our particular words?"

Everyone in the room turned to look at Sarah. At first Sarah was confused by this, but suddenly realized it was she who had spoken.

Dee looked up, and gazed around the room until his eyes met hers. He stared at her with contempt and disbelief. The other guests, her father included, stared in wonder at this young woman challenging the doctor's reputation as a sage and oracle of wisdom. It was not only disrespectful but audacious. Dr. Dee let out a half laugh and batted his hand at her as if trying to brush away a pesky fly.

"Those are only illusions of choice," he said dismissively. Again no one spoke against that belief.

No. No. He cannot be allowed to give his opinion without defending it, Sarah wanted to scream. She pressed on.

"Then, if a person commits a crime, how can the law hold him responsible for his actions, if, as you say, he had no choice?"

Dr. Dee, through liquid eyes that resembled the whites of an egg, smiled indulgently. "I am saying it is the divine plan for that person to break the law."

"Really? If we have no choice in how we behave, what is the purpose of prayer and contrition?" Sarah countered.

The doctor's face turned as stony as the side of a granite cliff. He glared at her. The room went dead silent while everyone waited to hear his reply.

Finally, he snapped, "Woman, these are greater mysteries than your female mind is capable of understanding."

Sarah's bile boiled up inside her. *What kind of answer was that? Dr. Dee would never have been so insulting if a man had challenged him.*

"Dr. Dee, you have not answered my question," Sarah snapped. "If it is God's will for me to speak my thoughts freely, then it is God who is waiting for you to tell us the purpose of prayer and contrition when every evil deed, according to you, is done with God's blessing."

The silence that followed was so complete that it appeared the whole world had stopped and was waiting for a response. Seconds went by. Nobody dared breathe. At long last Dee turned on his host and spat out the only response he had. "Who is this woman, Lord Dudley, who dares to challenge me, an advisor to the late queen?" Dr. Dee shouted. "How can you allow this, this half-wit pretending to be a scholar to remain under your roof?"

Lord Dudley's face turned purple, and his lips formed words but no sound came out. Sarah looked around at the noble faces, staring back at her, their eyes bulging and their mouths opened, as if struck dumb. She glanced at where her father was sitting among the imposing lords and ladies; his frame seemed to have shrunk down to the size of a child. There was a wild-eyed expression on his face. He shook his head ever so slightly and held his hands together as if in prayer. That was enough to give Sarah pause. She looked around the room with its magnificent architecture and at the wealthy and learned gathering and suddenly realized that Dr. Dee was right. It was she who was out of place in this great house, she who was pretending that her knowledge, gained through reading some books and engaging in discussions with a collection of mostly common folk, made her an equal among these great men and women. She could never be one of them.

With great effort, Sarah rose and stood tall, so everyone could see her scarred cheek, the only thing on her body that was not borrowed. In a strong, clear voice, she spoke to the assemblage.

"I apologize to all of you, especially to you, Dr. Dee, for my questions. They were reckless and thoughtless. Lord Dudley, you have been a most gracious host and I have been a most ungracious guest."

There was nothing left to do but to curtsy politely to the gathering and escape from the salon. Robert was sitting by the door, and as she moved past him, he gave her a slight nod and wink. She fled up the staircase and down the long hall to the last door on the left and into her sleeping quarters for the night. She was sorry she had engaged in a discussion with Dr. Dee or indeed had spoken at all. Perhaps it was the wine that had loosed her tongue. She had vowed not to utter a word and now she had embarrassed herself and her father, but she knew she was right. The others in the room were either dim-witted or cowed by such a personage as Dr. John Dee. How was he such an illustrious, spiritual visionary when he had no better retort than to imply that every female has a weak mind and is incapable of serious thought?

She considered what Lord Dudley and his prominent guests would think of her comments. How did they regard her now? Probably as a foolish, outspoken commoner who did not know her place and did not have the intellect to understand complex issues. Her remarks were exactly what she had promised herself not to say. What was the point of this visit, anyway? Why did Robert invite her? She felt as though she had entered a foreign land where the standards of behavior that she had been taught did not apply. She wanted to leave this extravagant home immediately and get away from these contemptible people who held beliefs that only mimicked what was popular at the time.

It seemed impossible to her that she could be so happy one moment and so distressed the next.

Chapter Eleven

November 1607
Tisbury Manor
The Proposal

Sarah was glad she was alone in her chambers and that her maid, Jane, was sleeping in an anteroom. She changed into a white linen nightgown but was too overwrought to go to bed. The window ledge offered her a seat that overlooked a garden. A cool breeze and the scent of pine filled her lungs and helped her to relax. Her heart was still pounding from her distress at having been insulted by such a pompous person as Dr. Dee in the company of Robert's family and friends. Her head was pounding as well from taking too much wine. It felt as if it was filled with thistles and burrs. She began to hear bits of conversation, men saying good night and the creak of doors being opened and shut outside in the hall. She remained at the window long after all the noises had died down. She thought about what it would be like to live in this large house with illustrious people coming and going.

Her reverie was disturbed by a soft knock on the door. *It must be Jane,* she thought, *with today's traveling clothes cleaned and pressed.*

"Come in."

She heard the squeak of the hinges as the door opened, and without turning to look, she said, "Just put the clothes on the table."

After a short pause, the door closed and Sarah returned to her thoughts.

"What a lovely garden," she murmured.

"I'm glad you like it," came a reply.

Sarah spun her head around and was startled to see Robert standing near her. He was casually dressed in breeches and a loose-fitting white shirt, with the silk scarf tied around his neck. His eyes were fixed on her partially opened nightgown. She put her hands to her breast and whispered, "You shouldn't be here."

"But you invited me in," he said sheepishly.

"I thought it was my maid. Robert, you need to leave."

"But I have to talk to you tonight. You ran out of the salon so fast. I want to tell you that you were wonderful. You put that pompous ass in his place. No one else would have dared to say what they were really thinking. I am so proud of you."

Sarah was pleased but a little perplexed. Proud? That is an intense feeling to have for someone you hardly know.

"Thank you, now go."

"I will, but first I have to talk to you. I am leaving early tomorrow on business for my father that will take most of the day. I tried to get him to send someone else, but Father insisted it had to be me. I will not have a chance to speak to you alone, and I need to ask you something." He paused long enough for Sarah's mind to try to conjure up what he could possibly have to ask her in private. She could think of nothing.

"Since my stay at your father's home, I have thought of you constantly. When I wake, you are there, scrutinizing me, your eyes full of doubt about my character and my intentions, but I have also seen a flicker of passion in those eyes and felt it on your lips."

Sarah felt a flush move from the tip of her head down to her toes. Their kiss in the grove did inflame her in ways she had never experienced before.

"It is hopeless for me to try to forget you," Robert continued softly. "My sister told me that I must be in love with you, and she is always right about such matters."

Sarah smiled at the very notion of such a feeling.

"So—" Robert took in a deep breath. "I must marry you, or I will kill myself. Which do you prefer?"

Sarah could not believe what her ears were hearing. The man was either mad or impulsive beyond belief. She wanted to burst out laughing at such an insane idea, but if he was mad, she did not want to upset him. Perhaps the cruel disappointment he suffered when Lady Anne died had unhinged him.

"I prefer that you go to your chambers and get some sleep. You must be suffering from exhaustion or perhaps you had too much to drink."

"Are you refusing me?" His voice cracked.

"Robert, I hardly know you, and our families are not equals. I…" The idea was so absurd that she did not know what else to say.

"Hear me out. I have tried to be obedient to the king, but his first choice of a bride for me became so sickly that she could not marry—thankfully. I then fell in love with Anne Herbert, the Countess of Pembroke's daughter, and I felt sure that King James would approve, since we were both from titled families, but just as the engagement was about to be announced, an elderly earl persuaded the king to give Anne to him. Anne was so distraught she fled to Cambridge and there contracted the ague. She died soon after." Robert's chest was heaving, and he raised his hands to cover his face. There was a silence that was broken by a pitiful moan. Finally Robert continued.

"You have all the qualities I want in a woman—knowledge, wit, boldness, charity, beauty, and passion. Those are enough to satisfy me for a lifetime. I can not wait any longer for the king to decide whom I should marry. I want to marry you, and the king be damned!"

Again there was a long silence. Sarah felt he would not leave unless she told him something that would push all thoughts of her being a possible wife out of his mind. She weighed how much she should tell him about her past. Reluctantly she uttered the words that she had heretofore only acknowledged in her head.

"It is impossible for me to have children, so no man will ever…I can never marry anyone."

"Why is that?"

Good God. Why does he persist with his questions? She bristled. She turned her head toward the window so he could not see the pain in her eyes.

"When I was fourteen," she began, "a stranger came to the Mews looking for my father who was not at home. He asked if I might give him some ale for he had come a long way and was very thirsty. His dress and manner indicated that he was high born and deserving of respect. My father had taught me to be hospitable to travelers, as you well know, so I asked him to wait outside while I went to fill a tankard. He followed me into the house, and started looking around, as if searching for something. I thought he wanted money and told him there was none. When he looked in my father's library, he shouted, 'This is proof enough. Your father is a traitor and needs to be punished.' He headed for the door, and then stopped, looked at me, and smiled. 'I will take you abed. That will be punishment enough.' Then he attacked me."

Sarah waited for Robert to speak, but he kept silent. He might as well know the worst then. She took a deep breath and continued.

"I fought back and had escaped his grasp, but he pulled out a knife and threatened to kill me if I did not give myself to him." Sarah paused, trying to control her voice. "I told him that I would rather be dead so…" Her voiced quavered, but she continued. "So he slashed my face and my belly. I fell to the floor, bleeding, and he ran out the door. Soon I lost consciousness, for how long I can not say. When I awoke, I was alone. I stayed on the floor, in a puddle of blood and shortly thereafter our old maid arrived. She was able to staunch the bleeding, having been trained by my father to treat wounds. She saved my life."

Sarah finally turned her head to look at Robert. She thought, now he will say how sorry he is for me and leave. Instead he bent down and kissed her forehead, and then the tip of her nose, the scar on her cheek, and finally her lips.

"Robert, don't you understand? The wounds were deep. I can never have children." The last few words came out in a half sob.

"I understand that I love you. I will take you as you are."

With that, he sat on the edge of the window ledge, facing her, holding her hands and sighing as he pressed his lips against her neck, and shoulders, and the cleavage of her breast. She tried to move her arms in protest, but they felt paralyzed.

Robert looked up and breathed softly, "I need to know. Will you marry me?"

Sarah leaned back and closed her eyes. *This has to be a dream,* she thought.

Chapter Twelve

November 1607
Tisbury Manor
A Surprising Discovery

Sarah opened her eyes to the sun streaming in the window and was startled by the lateness of the hour. She had always been an early riser; at home the roosters woke her each morning with their high-pitched crowing, but there were no sounds from fowl here; only strange voices that filtered into the room from far away. She sat up straight in bed and immediately put her hand on her head, feeling like she was in a fog. Never had she drunk as much wine, followed by brandy. She looked around, remembering where she was, inhaling the luxury of it all. The bed chamber was handsomely decorated with walls of warm green wallpaper and pink silk bed covers. She leaned back on the feather pillow and thought back to last night. What a strange dream she had. It must have been the wine and the excitement of the evening that made her mind take such a spin. She reddened with the thoughts of what she imagined took place. Shame on me for letting my thoughts be so lusty.

A knock on the door surprised her.

"Yes? Who is it?"

"Jane, Miss Sarah."

"You may come in."

"Are you feeling ill? You never sleep this late."

"No. Not really, but I do feel muddled... and sore."

"It was the long horseback ride you took with Miss Elizabeth yesterday, I'm sure. And from the looks of the bedcovers all twisted around, it looks like you did not sleep well."

Sarah looked astonished at the sheets wrapped around her. She had never mussed a bed like this.

"Yes, perhaps it was the ride. I don't usually ride a horse for so long. Yes, that must be it." She tried to appear calm, but her voice trembled.

"Well, Miss Sarah. Shall I prepare your bath now?"

"Oh, yes. Please do."

After Jane left the room, Sarah started to unwrap herself from the sheets. A bright object caught her eye. There, twisted in among the linen, was a familiar silk scarf. She laid back in bed and groaned.

"Dear God, what have I done?"

She stayed in bed for a while, replaying what events she could remember from the evening before. Every fiber in her body wished she could change the scene that she kept seeing in her mind. Eventually she made her way down the hall, hoping she would not meet anyone. The door to the bath was opened, and as she walked in, Jane was just putting the last bucket of hot water into the tub.

"I'll stay and wash your back, Miss Sarah."

"No, no. I'm fine. I want to just soak a while."

Jane nodded and left, shutting the door behind her. Sarah let the warm water ooze into all her pores. She needed time to be alone and think. *What was real and what was a dream?* In spite of being in the heated bathtub, a tremor went through her. *What sins have I committed? What will my father think of me if he ever finds out?* It was tempting to sink under the water and be done with life.

Just then the door opened without a knock and in strode Elizabeth in a fashionable silk outfit, looking jaunty and smiling mischievously.

"Good morning, Sarah. Isn't it a lovely day?"

Why is she so cheerful? Sarah thought. *She drank as much wine as I did. Maybe she is more used to it.* Without waiting for a reply, Elizabeth continued.

"I spoke to Robert early this morning. He was leaving to see some of our tenant farmers a half day's journey from here. He hopes to be back by nightfall. He said to tell you he will return as soon as possible."

Getting no reaction from Sarah, Elizabeth lowered her voice and continued. "He thought you were wonderful last night." Sarah still said nothing, but her face turned as hot as flames in a bonfire. *What exactly had Robert told his sister about last night?*

"So did I. Dr. Dee did not live up to his reputation as a sage. His rhetoric failed to convince anyone there. What an imposter. You should finish your bath quickly and get dressed. We have preparations to make."

"What preparations?"

"You and Robert are getting married within a month! That is not much time, but Robert insists that the wedding be here, of course. Father is not the least bit pleased because he wanted Robert to marry a kin or at least a noblewoman and he thinks you have too much spirit for your own good. But Father is very partial to Robert and depends on him to help run the estate while Edward is away, so, you see, they must come to some agreement. Come, let me help you out of the tub."

Sarah closed her eyes and tried to breathe. It was all real, all her memories of her and Robert in bed. And now Elizabeth would see the scars on her belly and would undoubtedly demand an explanation and surely tell her brother that on no account could he marry such a disfigured woman. She took Elizabeth's extended hand and stepped out of the tub. Without comment, Elizabeth took the linen towels and wiped Sarah's back and arms brusquely. She looked down at Sarah's belly.

"Do the scars hurt?" she asked.

"No. Not unless I have a tight garment on."

"Then put on something comfortable. We are going into town to choose material for your wedding dress."

Sarah did as she was told, letting Elizabeth dress her as she chose. Sarah felt dumbstruck; she could not think or talk. At breakfast, thankfully, only her father and Robert's mother, Lady Katherine, were present. Her father smiled at her and said warmly, "I am happy for you," but he looked worried. Robert's mother, who put custom and duty above all else, said nothing but her eyes bore into her so keenly that Sarah felt she was struck by lightning.

Lady Katherine held herself rigidly as if she was posing for a portrait. Only her hands moved, in and out, clenching and unclenching an invisible object. The tension was finally broken when her ladyship turned her head away and said, "We have been very worried about Robert since Anne died. He has been so lonely and melancholy since the loss of his beloved cousin. She was a lady of great pedigree and decorum as well as a thing of beauty."

She turned back to look at Sarah, her eyes resting on Sarah's left cheek. The implication was clear. Compared to Lady Anne Herbert, Sarah was unfit to be Robert's future bride.

"He seems determined to go through with this marriage, but I want to warn you, there is great danger in such a union." Her voice had the timbre of iron scraping against iron.

Sarah swallowed hard. Tears came to her eyes, and she could not speak. Nothing could change her face or her lineage or her character. For the first time in her life, she felt like a totally worthless person.

"Go now with Elizabeth. She will know exactly what you will need for your wedding day if it indeed takes place."

Chapter Thirteen

November 1607

Salisbury

Shopping for a Trousseau

Escaping from Lady Katherine was a relief, but the hustle and bustle of Salisbury made Sarah dizzy and nauseous. There were masses of people dressed in costumes of every color and design; hawkers and urchins stuck to her heels like burrs; there were dogs, cats, horses, pigs, chickens, and sheep who wandered around sniffing at everything and everyone. The bellows and brays from the beasts clashed with the calls and the chatter from the crowds; the stench of dung commingling with the reek of sweat was enough to make the two ladies flee indoors.

At a milliner's shop, Elizabeth bought yards of taffeta and satin, a gauzy veil, ruffs for around the neck and wrists, leather pumps, a cloak of peach satin, and gloves of the same color. Although Sarah was asked for her opinion on colors and fabric, she was too shaken to respond except with a nod. All the decisions were Elizabeth's who never inquired as to the cost. Their purchases were handed off to a servant who followed them from shop to shop. Next they arrived at a milliner's and bought several hats of velvet and silk. Then Elizabeth pushed Sarah into the shop of a goldsmith where Elizabeth purchased a high quality mirror. It was oval-shaped with gold edging.

"This is my wedding gift to you."

"Really, Elizabeth. That is much too expensive."

"Nonsense. It is my choice, so you have to accept it. And besides, it is father's money, not mine." She laughed at her own cleverness.

They passed by an apothecary shop, and Sarah asked to see inside. Wells had a very small shop; this one was four times the size. Its aisles contained shelves with row upon row of stoppered bottles each with a label: mercury, arsenic, clay powder, snake skins, snuff, plasters, hen's eggs, urine, blood. At first Sarah was impressed by the variety of herbal medicines available, but when she overheard the apothecary telling a customer to use boiling oil on a gunshot wound of a servant, she was appalled.

"You should first try wine and figwort for such an injury. Boiling oil is likely to cause more damage and not allow the wound to get air to heal itself."

The customer looked at her in disbelief, while the apothecary raised his eyebrows as high as they could go. What impudence coming from a woman!

"How do you know this, Madam?" the customer asked, enjoying the expression of the proprietor's face.

"My father is a respected doctor, and his skills are well-known."

"What do you say to that, Apothecary? Ever heard of it?"

The apothecary fidgeted with his bottles sitting on the counter, and then stared at Sarah's scar. Sarah stared right back. Finally he said, "I have heard of using wine and figwort, but I follow Doctor Compton's orders and he only recommends boiling oil. Says that is what is used in battle for gunshot wounds."

Sarah shook her head in disgust. Elizabeth, who was anxious to resume their journey, tugged at Sarah's arm and they quickly departed, leaving the customer to decide how to best treat the wound.

The two ladies walked into a seamstress shop that was tucked in between a draper and a glover. Sarah was measured for a long gown, and then she and Elizabeth discussed what design the gown would take. Elizabeth had a specific pattern in mind; she was quite knowledgeable about high fashion, having been to Court and elegant parties many times. Sarah let her sister-to-be make the final decision, feeling that Elizabeth had taken her under her wing and enjoyed showing her expertise to someone whom she must consider to be a simple country girl or worse.

As they proceeded down the main street, they passed a woman with a basket of lemons and oranges competing with children to see who could haggle with customers for the best price. There were onions, herbs, and lettuce in abundance, all being sold from street vendors who moved in and out of horse and cart traffic, burdened with their heavy wares. Sarah was assaulted by the unpleasant aromas of horse manure, fish brine, human sweat, rotten fruit, and some unidentifiable smells, all swirling around her in a vortex of stench. She wanted to go back to the peace and comfort of her own house or seclude herself in the bedroom at the Dudley estate. But Elizabeth had other thoughts.

"Now we must dine at The Old Mill where the owner knows me and will seat us so we have a view of the river. His mince pies and custard tarts are the best in the city."

Sarah, who had been so nervous at breakfast that she had eaten only a fig, would have been satisfied with a piece of smoked salmon at the fishmonger's stall they were passing. The two ladies reached the inn just as Sarah's legs were giving out. The lunch was interrupted by some young men who came over to their table to chat. Elizabeth introduced them to

Sarah and flirted with them under the watchful eyes of her coachman and the owner. It occurred to Sarah that Robert's sister knew these gentlemen were to be at this inn and she was enjoying as much banter with them as propriety would allow. The shopping expedition had been an excuse for her to leave the manor where she was kept under her parents' thumb.

When they headed back to the house with their purchases stowed behind the coachman, Sarah sat quietly while Elizabeth chatted away about the qualities of each of the young gentlemen she had encountered in the inn.

"When I marry, it shall be to a man that I can abide. I am content to wait, for the older I get, the closer in age I will be to whomever the King approves."

Sarah smiled at her friend's light-hearted mood while she pondered her own uncertain future. The excitement and joy of marriage had quite suddenly changed to dread and foreboding. His parents were vehemently against a union between her and Robert. To begin a marriage with such parental displeasure was not what she had anticipated. They were heading into a dark and dangerous tunnel with no light at the end.

Chapter Fourteen

November 1607

Tisbury Manor

A Conversation with a Guest

"Look at what we have bought for Sarah's wedding," exclaimed Elizabeth. She and Sarah came into a sitting room where Lady Katherine and Lady Mary Sidney were conversing. While they displayed their purchases to the ladies, Sarah noticed a troubled look on both women's faces. Lady Katherine asked Elizabeth to come with her for she had something to discuss, and when she protested, her mother practically pushed her out of the room.

Sarah was left alone in the presence of Lady Mary, the Countess of Pembroke, a widow, and as Sarah had been told, a mother whose daughter had died suddenly last year. Elizabeth confided to Sarah that Lady Mary was an accomplished poet, writer, and musician as well as a lover of science. What should Sarah, a commoner from a small village, say to her?

Sarah smiled at the handsome countess whose bright blue eyes radiated intelligence and wit. The countess said nothing but seemed to be sizing her up. Sarah looked around the room for some inspiration. Finally, she stammered, "I have read some sonnets by your brother, Sir Philip Sidney. I enjoyed them very much."

The countess raised her eyebrows. "You have read Philip's sonnets? He was my dear brother who was killed in a war in the Netherlands."

"I am sorry to hear that."

"His death was a great loss to me. We were very close, and we collaborated on several works of poetry. Do you write verses?"

"Oh, no, Lady Mary. But I love to read. My father has brought home many books on many subjects, but sometimes it is a challenge for me to understand them."

"Tis a pity that you had no opportunity to be tutored, but you have learned much by reading and by observing. Your father has told us that you are a great help to him in caring for the people in your village. How do you treat for burns?"

"I put wine on burns, which helps to take the sting out and also helps to hasten the healing." Sarah answered forthrightly, hoping that Lady Mary would approve of this method.

"Wine can be used if there is nothing else, but we have found vinegar to be more effective, especially in stopping infection."

"Oh, I will certainly try that, Lady Mary. Thank you. I have read a book called *The Good Housewife's Jewell,* which gives many recipes for helping to cure common ailments."

"Yes. I have a copy of that book. I have concocted some recipes of my own as well—a medicine for the cough, another to kill worms, one for sore eyes, and many others. It is a pastime of mine. Your father said that he had hundreds of books in his library on many different subjects."

"Yes, but it is the books on medicine that I find most interesting. I study them faithfully and wish I could use my knowledge to heal people as my father does. Of course," she said looking down and blushing, "it is a foolish desire. I cannot change my sex or my situation in life." She paused as if wondering how to proceed.

Mary nodded sympathetically. "Yes, I understand exactly how you feel." Sarah was surprised. She had not expected a member of the nobility to be so empathetic.

"I, too, have had to endure disappointment and intolerance because I am a woman and now a widow. What is men's right by their sex is women's wrong because of theirs. We must have the heart of a tiger to endure the injustice."

How comforting and encouraging, thought Sarah. *Lady Mary is truly a remarkable woman.*

Now the countess addressed the events of the past evening. "I was taken aback by your comments to Dr. Dee last night."

Sarah reddened, and prepared herself for a dressing down.

"You took on a formidable opponent, someone whose training and intellect are extensive in many ways, but narrow when it comes to debating with women. You remind me so much of my daughter Anne who died last year from a reoccurring illness. She was curious, talented, and clever. Did you know that she and Robert were secretly engaged, but their marriage was not approved by King James?"

Sarah feigned surprise. "Not approved?"

"That is correct. The king must approve of all marriages by the nobility. It broke Anne's heart, and I feel it hastened her death. Robert is a very courtly man, and I admire his intelligence and pluck. You are a woman with knowledge and spirit but still a commoner. I fear Robert has not thought through this hasty marriage. The king will not consent to your wedding. If Robert persists, he will be imprisoned…unless…"

Lady Mary paused and then, in a soft voice, continued. "If you both disappear, then the king is powerless to stop you."

"Disappear? Where could we go that the king could not find us?"

"You might sail to France. Lord and Lady Dudley would not like it, but Robert has suffered from two failed engagements. They have been worried about his being in ill humor for so long; they feared he would die by his own hand."

"Then our marriage must be done in secret?"

"I believe so. I think you and Robert must go before the king finds out because then he will immediately know why you both have disappeared and come after you. If you leave at once, he will not know you have left until you both are safely away. Do you speak French?"

"A little. I learned some words and phrases from visitors to our home and from reading books they left in trade."

"Then France may be a good place for you both. But be on guard; do not trust the air with secrets for a spy of the king may be near. I know of someone who has left her home and is safely in hiding, but in that case, it was she who was told to marry a much older man, one several times her age. This she would not do. But, of course, it is easier for a titled woman to hide than it is for a titled man."

"Is Robert aware that we must go away? He told me none of this." Sarah's words came out in a rush, and her voice betrayed her agitation.

"I believe he feels that he has done his best to serve the king and that the king will approve this union, but King James has never shown any such sympathy. Robert is still very angry with King James for not approving of his betrothal to Anne. Several years ago, he obeyed the king's wishes and became engaged to a sickly woman in whom he had no interest and waited over a year for her health to improve. When it didn't, and the engagement was called off, he felt sure that his marriage to Anne would be welcomed since they are distant cousins. Now Robert is determined to marry you and does not worry about getting King James' approval. That will be very dangerous for you both."

Sarah noticed that Lady Mary said "are distant cousins," not "were," but did not attempt to correct her, thinking it must be difficult to lose a child in the bloom of youth. How Mary must miss her last surviving daughter.

"How old was Anne when she died?"

"She was just three and twenty and so full of life." The eyes of the countess filled up, and her lips trembled.

"But you said she was sick?"

Mary composed herself before answering. "It was quite a sudden death, but she did have reoccurring bouts with the ague. She hated to miss the masques and court ceremonies, so she attended in spite of her ill-health."

Sarah tried to remember if Robert had ever mentioned Anne being ill. She was sure he hadn't, and yet Anne had died from a persistent illness. She could not figure out how Anne could be so sickly and yet so healthy as to attend balls and masques. Apparently Robert did not take Anne's illness seriously; otherwise Anne's death would not have been a shock.

"I have never been to a masque, but I do love to attend plays. My father has taken me to several, whenever we have visited London."

"Which play is your favorite?"

"*Romeo and Juliet.*"

"Oh, that is Anne's favorite, too."

Again Lady Mary used the present tense. *Perhaps*, Sarah thought, *Lady Mary still thinks of her daughter as alive.*

"I will talk to Robert when he returns about what we should do. I hate the thought of leaving my father forever without either of us having any news of the other."

Lady Mary eyed this commoner with curiosity and pity, and then rose and stood erect, looking every inch like a queen about to address her subjects. Sarah hurriedly got up and waited for the countess to speak. Lady Mary beckoned her to come closer. When they were within whispering distance, Lady Mary murmured, "I have devised a way to communicate in code, which I will relate to you in writing. It must be kept secret, or all will be discovered and you and Robert will be imprisoned."

"That is most generous of you. I am in your debt."

"Whether we shall meet again, I know not. I bid you my everlasting farewell."

Sarah had never heard such sincere and heartfelt words of parting. "My Lady, I shall never forget your kindness." Sarah remembered to curtsy and watched with sadness as the countess gathered her skirts and, with regal bearing and grace, left the sitting room. *What a clever and courtly woman,* Sarah concluded. *I have learned so much from her in a very short time. I wish I could have spoken to her longer.*

But when she thought about what lay ahead, her mind was filled with fear and misgivings. What had made her so happy last night now seemed like a curse which would bring her nothing but pain and sorrow.

Chapter Fifteen

November 1607
Tisbury Estate
Lost and Confused

Sarah could not make sense of all that Lady Mary had confided to her. She left the dining room, rushed to her chamber, and threw herself on the bed. Why hadn't Robert told her what their marriage would entail? How could he be so thoughtless and reckless? She considered the choices now in front of her. *If I marry Robert, I must leave my father forever and go to live in a strange country. If I do not marry Robert, there is little likelihood that I will ever marry any man as learned and loving as he is.* She decided that she needed to talk this over with someone. Her father would not be able to step back and look at her situation objectively, knowing that if she and Robert went to France, he would never see her again. There was only one other person here she trusted who could advise her—Elizabeth—although she, too, could not be totally objective.

As Sarah was about to leave the chamber, she found a letter that had been slipped under the door. It was from Mary Sidney and contained the musical code to use as a secret means of communication. She left it on a chest and went looking for Elizabeth, but she was nowhere to be found. *I will go for a long walk,* she thought. *That always helps me to calm down and think.* The grounds were enormous, and she could easily get lost, so she decided to head in only one direction. As she walked, she imagined the excitement and challenge of living in a foreign country, meeting travelers and natives of France, tasting different foods, seeing magnificent cathedrals. She smiled at all the possibilities before her until she remembered her father. He was her only family and had brought her up almost by himself. She loved him more than anyone. How could she leave him, at his advanced age, knowing she would never see him again? She could not make such a momentous decision all alone. Where was Robert when she needed him most for comfort and reassurance?

She came to the end of the lane and stopped. In front of her were two paths. She stood still for a long while, hesitating. *I cannot even decide on what path to take in these gardens; how can I decide on what to do for the rest of my life?* She was so angry with herself, she swore. *Damn King James, damn Dr. Dee, and damn Lord Dudley. I am tired of having to obey men of great power and little sense.* Looking down each lane, she decided to take paths that led to the right so that on her way back, she would do the opposite. Again, that was only possible when there were two choices. A while later, three lanes appeared. The one on the right went up a steep hill. The middle path led into a thick grove of fruit trees. On the left, the path was winding and she could not see where it would take her. Which one should she choose? Exhausted and confused, she turned around to head back and saw a rider on horseback galloping toward her. Her heart skipped a beat. Maybe it was Robert! As the rider drew closer, she saw that it was an older man and finally recognized him as Robert's father, Lord Dudley.

"Don't you see the sky darkening?" Lord Dudley shouted. "And why are you walking by yourself? Have you no sense, girl?"

He sounded just like Robert at the Mews, yelling at her over something she did not find the least bit wrong. His demeanor was apparently typical of noblemen who were used to taking out their displeasure on a woman. She did not like being scolded like a child and was ready to snap back, but it occurred to her that this man might soon be her father-in-law.

"Sir, I could find no one to walk with me. I will return directly."

"You will never get back to the manor before the storm sets in. Give me your hand and climb up behind me."

Sarah did as she was told and together they raced toward the manor, taking so many twists and turns that Sarah began to think he was confused himself. The great house finally appeared over a hill just as the rain started to beat down on them. By the time the horse pulled up to the front steps, they were both thoroughly soaked. Sarah quickly slid down and raced for the door, while a servant came to take the reins and to hand Lord Dudley a cloak to protect himself.

She stood in the hall and waited for him, thinking of what she could say that would be an acceptable excuse for wandering so far. As soon as Lord Dudley entered and saw her still there, soaking wet, he exclaimed, "What is the matter with you? Get on some dry clothes before you catch cold."

"But, sir, I wanted to explain."

"You are a foolish, headstrong girl. How my son can be so besotted with you is beyond belief." He turned and strode down the long hall with a servant close behind, wiping up the floor as water dripped from his clothes. Sarah stayed where she was, watching him until he disappeared. Any hope of marrying Robert disappeared as well. *Damn him,* she thought. *If this is how all members of the upper class treat women, I want no part of it.* Another servant urged her over to the staircase and to her bedchamber, anxious to wipe away the water that had no business being on the ornate floor. Slowly she climbed the marble steps, her mind mulling over Lord Dudley's words: foolish and headstrong. *That is what I am,* she thought, *at least in Robert's world. Back at the Mews, I was admired by everyone I came in contact with. Well, perhaps not the squire.* She smiled at the memory of his bile and bluster, trying to save face in front of his neighbors while she dared him to deny that poor people were dying daily from starvation. When she arrived at her chambers and started to remove the wet garments, she had made her decision. *I must tell Robert that I cannot marry him.*

Chapter Sixteen

November 1607
Tisbury Manor
Escape

Robert would have none of it.

"Sarah, *you are not marrying my family; you are marrying me.* Even if my parents were happy with my choice of wife, we can not live here. Let us go to my father and have this matter out once and for all."

Robert practically dragged Sarah into a sitting room where Lord Dudley was at his leisure, holding a pipe in one hand while perusing a letter in the other. The acrid smoke made Sarah wince and cough; it was a habit that only the wealthy could afford, and she wondered what possible pleasure they got from it.

Lord Dudley looked up when they entered, and before Robert could utter a word, he said, "I hope you are not going to ask for my blessing. I have made my feelings—"

"But Father, it is my life and I have found someone I want to marry," he shouted. "I have lost two potential brides trying to do your bidding and—"

"It is the king's bidding, you fool! He is the one who can have you thrown in prison for not marrying a noblewoman."

"Father," said Robert, in a quieter tone, "I am now twenty-six and have been without a woman my entire life. It is time I married, and if the king does not consent, then I will do so secretly and live out my days in hiding."

"Do you realize what your future will hold? You will be hunted down like a criminal, and when you are caught, you will be sent to the Tower. It is a folly to think otherwise. Is this woman worth such a price?"

Robert looked at Sarah with adoration. "Yes, most assuredly yes!" He took her hand and pressed it to his lips and breathed, "You are everything I ever wanted in a woman."

His father's eyes became moist. "Then I shall never see or hear from you again. Even sending me a letter could be dangerous. Is this how you want the rest of your life to be? Living in fear and hiding from everyone you know?"

"Hiding is not what I want, but it is what must be."

"Where will you go? What will you live on?"

"To France, as Lady Sidney suggested. The king's men will never find us there. And with my education, I know that I will find some suitable occupation."

"Then if that is your decision, I wish you well. Edward would certainly not approve. Right now he is out beating the bushes trying to find someone to arrest. Papists, plotters, anyone that he thinks will give him favor with the king. Thank God he is not here, or he would stop you or even worse, tell the king what you intend to do. You do not have much of an inheritance, but I suppose I will have to give you some funds to get you safely away. The rest is up to you. People are going to ask about you. What should I tell them?"

"Only that I cannot shake off my grief about Anne's death and am shut up in this manor. If the king sends some of his men to look for me, tell them that I ran off."

Robert watched his father turn and walk away—a father so distraught that he could not embrace his son one last time. But Elizabeth did embrace him and Sarah, tearfully wishing them God's speed and proclaiming that they would meet again.

"It cannot be that we shall never laugh or quarrel with each other again. I forbid it. Find a way to let me know where you are, and I will stow away on a ship bound for France."

Her words were silly as they all knew, but the three of them laughed at such an impossible scheme. Besides her father, Sarah was going to miss Elizabeth the most. In so short a time, the two young women had become as close as blood sisters.

Of course, there could not be a wedding in Salisbury; word of it would reach the king within days. Sarah insisted that she and Robert accompany her father back to the Mews and then make further plans. She could not leave her father so abruptly. John Burton was grateful to have the company of his daughter and future son-in-law, but could take no joy in this marriage. Having a daughter living in another country was like having no daughter at all.

The local pastor in the area agreed to marry Robert and Sarah with only her father present. The pastor had known Dr. Burton all his life, and his own family had suffered many bouts of illness but had always recovered from them, thanks to the doctor's good care. The pastor felt he was repaying John Burton for keeping his family well. The trousseau that Elizabeth had planned for Sarah to wear was now not needed or wanted. Sarah dressed in a simple pale blue linen gown and a flowered petticoat, traditional among brides in rural areas. She did not want to attract the attention of passersby. She also wore a veil to hide her face and hair, hoping to avoid detection. Robert's attire was more elaborate but still in keeping with the need to appear ordinary. His light brown breeches and doublet with white linen shirt was modest for his aristocratic background. He, too, covered his head with a wide brimmed hat that hid most of his face.

The pastor kept the ceremony short and simple, nothing like what Elizabeth had imagined for them, but their vows were the same as if they had stood in the magnificent Salisbury Cathedral and swore their love and fidelity to each other there.

Chapter Seventeen

December 1607–March 1608
The Mews
Sarah's Secret

Now that Robert had the means to leave England and sail to France, the next difficulty was in doing it without the king's knowledge.

"Getting on a passenger ship and sailing safely to France is not going to be easy," Dr. Burton warned him. "The king is sure to send a message to sea captains commanding them to be on the lookout for a young couple."

"Then we must travel to France on a small boat. The distance between Dover and Calais is less than twenty-five miles. I will send a letter to my good friend who lives in Dover and ask him to find a small boat, perhaps a barque or a ketch, that can take two passengers from Dover to Calais as soon as possible."

While he and Sarah awaited a reply, John Burton sent letters to members of his academy saying that he would not be holding meetings for a while. He explained that he was suffering from fatigue and fever. The three of them stayed indoors mostly, spending many nights discussing possible occupations that Robert could take up in France. Anything involving the French nobility, like an interpreter or agent, was out of the question. King James would certainly hear of it. Robert had no interest in becoming a military man. The most appealing position was in academia, tutoring children of the wealthy or those of men in trade, or translating documents for French businessmen. Whatever he did, had to be done undercover, using an alias.

"Robert, let's go for a walk in the garden. I feel like a caged animal in here, and I have something I want to tell you in private," Sarah said.

"I suppose we must get outdoors sometime. We should walk in the woods where we cannot be seen."

Together they left the house by the back door and moved toward the distant grove of trees.

Robert began. "Time has gone by slowly indeed. Over a month and no word from Dover, and I am sorry I did not have a chance to say goodbye to my brother Edward. I may never see him again."

"Robert, tell me about him. Your father said that if Edward knew what you were doing, he might tell King James himself."

"Yes, he did say that, but I can't believe Edward would actually do that. His main occupation for many years has been to root out Papists in order to cozy up to the king. He told me he has found secret groups all over England, even in this county of Somerset."

A slight shiver ran down Sarah's back.

"Really! He came to this area. When was that?"

"Oh, it was years ago. Right after the Parliament approved the Act against Papists in the early 1590's. It was Queen Elizabeth's doing, and she generously rewarded those who discovered Catholic groups plotting against the Crown."

Sarah said nothing for a while. Finally, she managed to murmur, "And was your brother so rewarded?"

"I believe so. Not with titles as much as with money or sometimes a fine piece of jewelry."

She stopped walking and scrutinized his face, as if trying to discover something there that had escaped her notice.

"What is it, Sarah? You look pale."

"Like a necklace?" she said breathlessly.

"Yes. He was given a very fine necklace of gold and onyx. Why do you ask?"

A low groan escaped her lips.

"Have you seen such a fellow in these parts where everyone knows each other? I am sure such a stranger would be remembered."

"Oh, yes. Most definitely," she said, almost in a whisper. "I feel weak. I want to go back."

"But we have hardly been outside five minutes. You said you had something to tell me. Let's just get to the woods, and there you can rest."

As he was leading her to a nearby copse, they saw movement in the trees. Startled, they stopped and stared. They waited but did not see anything more.

"I think this hiding out has me spooked," said Robert. "I could have sworn I saw a person just there." He pointed to the copse about fifty feet away. "It was probably just the wind in the trees."

"Please let us go back. I need to sit down."

They turned around and headed back to the house, looking behind them for any sign of movement. Sarah walked through the rear door and went immediately to the staircase.

"I am tired and want to lie down."

Robert thought it must be that time of month. He went over to sit by Dr. Burton in front of the fireplace. Peter came in holding a broken stirrup.

"Sir, do you think this can be fixed?"

While Dr. Burton examined the leather binding, Robert asked Peter if he happened to have seen a stranger around the garden or woods recently.

"No, sir, just the sheriff looking for poachers."

"When was that?"

"Just a short while ago."

"Where exactly was he?"

"On the edge of the woods."

Robert looked at Dr. Burton with alarm. He blurted out, "I saw movement in the trees just now. The sheriff must have seen me and Sarah walking towards him. He certainly has heard that I am being hunted and will report me to the king's spymaster. Damn, what bad luck!"

Dr. Burton's hands shook as he handed the stirrup back to Peter.

"The leather is worn. Cut it off, and we will replace it. Be off now."

After Peter had left, Dr. Burton said, "You need to remember to hold your tongue in front of others."

"But Peter wouldn't talk. I have been very kind to him."

"He might be made to talk. That is the danger."

"Dr. Burton, forgive me. You are right. Now I must speak to Sarah."

Robert bolted up the stairs and found his wife staring at herself in the gilt-edged hand mirror that Elizabeth had insisted she keep. "Sarah, I must leave here quickly. Peter saw the sheriff in the woods just now. If the king's spies come looking for me, I am done for. What is the matter? You look like you have been crying."

"It is nothing. Just a headache. I need to lie down to rest." She turned away from him and stared out the window.

"But you must hear me out. The sheriff knows that I am here. I must get away."

"Robert, I believe…I believe that…" She fell on the bed and started to sob, her shoulders shaking uncontrollably.

Robert bent over her and whispered, "You cannot let this upset you so. I will make my way to the coast and find a place to stay. Then I will send for you."

"Please leave me be for just a little while," she cried.

"If you insist. I will speak to your father about an escape route and other particulars."

Sarah lay on the bed, numb to the wind blowing against the windowpane, numb to the voices downstairs, numb to every thought but one—her attacker was Robert's brother! Everything she had learned about Edward confirmed to her that he was the person who violently attacked her many years ago. It was inconceivable that two brothers could be so opposite in character. What was she to do now?

An hour later, Sarah descended the stairs and found her husband and her father huddled over a map of England. She went over to them and kissed her father on the cheek.

"Are you feeling any better, Daughter?" he asked.

"I have come to a decision."

"What decision?" Robert cut in. "You have nothing to decide." She ignored the question and continued on.

"Robert, if you leave, then I am coming with you."

"No, I should go alone. It will be easier and safer. I could sleep in the woods or under haystacks if I have to."

Sarah's eyes filled up. "No, no, no! This is not what we planned. I must go with you."

"But why? Once I am at the coast, I will send for you and have someone bring you to where I am hidden. It will be safer for you."

"Robert, you cannot leave without me because I believe I am with child."

Robert's lips moved, softly repeating the words "with child." He stared in disbelief, trying to understand what that meant.

"I thought—"

"I did not believe I could conceive after the knife attack did so much damage to my belly. Now it appears that I am able to carry a babe. If we have a child, he is not going to be born without his father being there. Don't you see? The longer I wait, the harder it will be for me to travel, and I can't bear to be away from you for who knows how long, not knowing what is happening to you."

She reached for him, and he hugged her close.

"Oh, Sarah, I am so happy but so frightened. This news changes everything. You are right. We must leave together for the sake of our child."

Her father was elated. He was going to have a grandchild, after all. He made her promise that some day she would return to the Mews so he could see the baby.

"Of course, we shall come back. This journey to France is to escape our present danger. In the future, things will improve and we will return to England." Sarah wanted, rather than believed that to be true.

Chapter Eighteen

March 1608
Southeast England
The Journey

They decided to leave just before dawn the next day, while it was still dark outside. It was early spring, a time when long trips were difficult because of the cold weather and the certain rain, which would make the roads muddy and slippery. They were to go on horseback, the fastest and safest way for two people to travel, but also a difficult ride for a pregnant woman who was pretending to be a young man.

Saying goodbye to Sarah's father was even more difficult. John Burton's eyes were red, and the dark circles under them made him look frightful.

"I know in my head that this move is necessary, but my heart is sick. Daughter, your happiness is worth more to me than your presence here. I will pray that some day we can be together again."

"We will reunite. We will! I will make it happen." Sarah's words were filled with such hope and spirit that her father's spirits lifted and he managed a warm smile.

Sarah came close to kiss him goodbye. "And, Father," she whispered softly, "don't forget to keep the code I gave you well hidden. Take it out only when you receive an unsigned letter."

His daughter, now wearing his cloak and breeches as a disguise, had donned one of Peter's caps over her pinned-up hair. She was barely recognizable even to her father, for now she looked every inch like a male servant. Having the scar on her face was an asset; it made her appear like a rough-and-tumble young man who got into fights. Robert wore clothes fit more for a yeoman than a nobleman; his worn leather breeches and a plain linen shirt were from Dr. Burton's servant, Jack, who was about the same size. Sarah had to travel astride her horse of course, pretending to be such a servant. Only Robert would talk with any strangers they met, as was proper. The distance they had to go was almost two hundred miles, four days' journey at best.

The first night they stopped outside of Southampton, a distance of more than fifty miles. They had pushed the horses to the limit, because the weather was pleasant and they were fit and hearty. At a small inn, Robert gave the innkeeper false identities. Sarah followed close behind as Robert climbed the stairs to their chamber, hoping that her posture and step were manly enough to fool the proprietors. They ate a meal of bread, meat, and ale in bed and fell asleep soon after, still in their riding clothes.

The next day broke cold and blustery. They got almost as far as Brighton, another fifty miles. Sarah tried not to show how sore her thighs were as she stumbled behind her "master" up to a small room in the eaves of the lodging house. This day's ride had been much more difficult because they were traveling along the coast, with wind and cold ripping through their clothes. They had come face to face with a constable who scrutinized them closely. He asked them for their papers, and Robert showed him a letter that John Burton had given him, directing him to purchase certain goods from an establishment in Folkestone, at least another day's ride. Satisfied, he allowed them to continue.

They retired almost as soon as they swallowed their last bite of bread and woke up much later than they had hoped. It was nearly two hours after dawn. Sarah's back ached, and her thighs were too painful to touch. She wanted to stay in bed all day. Robert was in better shape, but he too craved more rest. They heard the wind whistling and moaning through the trees outside their garret, giving them the shivers at the thought of leaving the warmth of the inn. Even worse, it had begun to rain hard and showed no signs of letting up. They decided to wait a while and at least get some added rest. Two hours later they came down to breakfast. While they were eating, Sarah noticed the proprietress watching her closely. She quickly began to chew her food with her mouth open, and spread her legs wide. After a moment, the woman looked away, apparently satisfied that Sarah was indeed a man servant.

At midmorning, with the storm still in full force, they had no choice but to continue their journey. By nightfall, they were just beyond Hurst Green, making only thirty miles that day. By keeping away from the coast, they felt more protected from the elements and from detection. In this village there was only one small house that had a sign offering accommodations. This type of inn had one big advantage: the owners would most likely have not been alerted to Robert Dudley's disappearance. However, the proprietors would also have the opportunity to scrutinize Robert and Sarah closely, having few guests to distract them, and Robert and Sarah were sure that the owners would question them at length. They were too wet and tired to worry about anything but eating supper and getting into bed.

As soon as they walked in, Robert knew he had made a mistake. The owner was also a constable and was suspicious at once. Why were they traveling in this weather? Where had they come from? What was the name of the person in Folkestone that they were to see? Robert gave him a made-up name and got a questioning look in return. Having no choice but to stay, Robert paid in advance for their meals and one night's lodging and they took seats at the table. While they attempted to eat supper, the questions continued nonstop.

What is the nature of your master's business? Why are you traveling so far at this time of year? Why not purchase these goods in London, which is much closer to your master's home?

So many questions made Sarah so nervous that she could not finish her supper and she wrapped a piece of meat in cloth to be eaten later. When they finally made their goodnights and reached their rooms, Robert told his wife that they must not stay the night. He was certain this constable would try to detain them in the morning so that he could check out their story. Fortunately, their chamber was a corner room with a view of the barn where their horses were stabled. For several hours they slept restlessly and awoke in pitch darkness. There was only a sliver of a moon, but the skies had finally cleared. Robert fashioned a rope out of bedsheets and they shimmied down the side of the building with their saddlebags on their shoulders. They were crossing an open area that led to the barn when they heard a low growl. They turned and looked into the face of the constable's large mastiff, black as the night, approaching from the rear of the inn. There was no escape. Sarah pressed a hand to her chest in fear. What could they do? They had come so far and were within a day of their goal. The dog was moving closer, and its growls became deeper. If only they could somehow distract it. She remembered the uneaten piece of meat from last night's supper, stuffed in her saddlebag. She quickly retrieved it and threw it close to the dog. It went for the bait and the two fugitives sped to the barn, swung up on their horses, and fled.

They had only forty miles to go, forty miles to Dover and a boat that went to France and safety. After several miles, they came to a fork. The left road was more like a path, while the right one was wide with deep ruts from wagons and carriages. As a precaution they decided on the road less traveled. It would be longer, but eventually they would come very close to Dover and the boat to France. If the constable checked with officials in the coastal towns, he would get no information about them.

Late on the fourth day of travel they arrived in Dover, a port town with an inner harbor to protect the boats from being swept into its cliffs. There had been a tremendous earthquake in the straits about a half century ago, with much devastation, forcing the inhabitants to rebuild their homes. Instead of the maze of lanes and alleys common to most small towns, the burghers of Dover designed long streets with similar-looking houses in straight rows on each side, like soldiers standing at attention. They rode slowly through the town, looking for somewhere to stop and rest. A weak moon was looking down on them, which kept them largely hidden. Now the most dangerous part of their flight began. Robert needed to make contact with his friend who would surely help them in finding passage to France, but now they needed a safe place to spend the night in this populated area.

In the distance they could see Dover Castle, high up on an earthen mound, built with twenty-foot walls to protect England from invaders and still manned by armed guards. If the fugitives were discovered here, a troop of soldiers was readily available to escort them back to London. A small dark house with a hand-painted sign reading Blackstone Inn came into view. Just as their horses were abreast with the front door, a muffled voice was heard.

"Good ev'en, Robert."

He spun around to see his friend leaning against a large oak tree, smiling. Thomas, a fellow student under the tutelage of the schoolmaster in the Dudley household, had studied and played together with Robert as young lads. They had become fast friends and trusted each other with their lives. Thomas had moved to Dover to oversee his father's shipping business and knew almost everyone in town. He gave them assurance that they could stay at this inn in safety as long as they remained out of sight. A small boat was to sail for Calais, just twenty-three miles away, in two days.

"How did you know we would be arriving today?" Robert asked.

"I didn't. I heard that the local constable was warned to detain you and your servant, or rather wife if he spotted you, so I have been on the lookout for two nights."

"You are a true friend indeed. I hope I can repay you some day."

"Of course. When I am on the run, I will send for you," he joked. "Keep hidden until Thursday eve when I will smuggle you in a cart to the dock. Once there I will take you and your wife to the boat."

"We are so tired that we could sleep for a fortnight," Robert replied. He and Sarah rejoiced that they had two whole days to rest. She was feeling poorly and feared that such hard travel on horseback would terminate her pregnancy. That night and well into the next morning they slept so soundly that neither the cocking of the crows nor the screeching of wagon wheels passing close to the house aroused them. As a precaution, they ate in their chamber and soothed each other's aches with liniment while discussing how they might survive in France. Robert was well educated in many areas, including knowledge of French and Spanish, making him a useful hire as long as his real identity was kept hidden. He decided to wait to see how things developed before committing himself to a trade.

Chapter Nineteen

April 1608
English Channel
The Voyage to Rouen

Sarah had never been on the English Channel. She had traveled less than one hundred miles from the Mews and that was to London to see the burial procession for Queen Elizabeth in 1603. Then it seemed all of England was at Westminster Abbey to mourn their beloved queen. Sarah's eyes had followed the trail of a thousand mourners moving in unison behind the casket, noblewomen in splendid gilded carriages, faithful soldiers on magnificent steeds, and the ragtag masses on foot bringing up the rear. The brilliant colored banners and coat of arms, and toots of the fife, the drum beats and bright lilies and daffodils strewn along the streets made an indelible imprint in her memory. From that time on, she had ached to travel far and wide, to swallow up the whole of the world, but accepting the truth that she was destined to see it only through books.

The forty-foot ketch left Dover at dawn. Sarah could see the white cliffs reflected in the early light as the boat pulled away from the dock and headed across the sea to France. The captain maintained a small crew of five and carried cargo along with three other travelers who were anxious to get back home. The Frenchmen complained all the way across the water about the terrible English weather and the even more terrible

English food. Robert, who had studied French as part of his schooling as a nobleman, struck up a conversation with these travelers and received much useful information. They came from Rouen, only eighty miles from Paris and where twelve years before, the college of Bourbon had been established. All three men were in the textile trade and were returning from a visit to London, having successfully arranged to export French fabrics into the waiting hands of clothiers, tailors, and drapers. As for Robert, he, now Robert Pennyman, told these businessmen amusing stories from his imagined childhood. He proved to be so engaging and colorful that when Robert explained that he and his wife were moving to France because she was in ill health from the cold climate of England, the travelers nodded their heads in sympathy and offered to help him resettle by providing the names of several notable businessmen in Rouen with whom he might find employment. They even wrote a letter of recommendation for him to show to these associates.

When they disembarked in Calais, Robert and Sarah Dudley engaged a carriage that would take them to Rouen. They spent the night in a small village called Abbeville where they ate a French meal of fish, bread, and wine. It was the first time in their four-month-old marriage that they were truly on their own and they felt like young lovers sneaking off to be by themselves. The next day they continued their journey through open fields, forests, and tiny villages until at last they saw the spires of the cathedral in Rouen appear in the distance. Its enormous height seemed to scrape the sky, as did their spirits. *How clever we are,* they both agreed.

Chapter Twenty

April 1608
Rouen, France

The Lay of the Land

And so began Robert and Sarah's exile. Never had they lived in such a large city, nearly sixty thousand, and with such a mixture of people, trades, and religions. Sailors swaggered along the docks of the Seine River, dodging passengers and carts full of cargo, coming and going by ship; textile merchants had shops closer to the city center whose half-timbered buildings seemed to sprout upwards in all directions like drunken sailors leaning upon each other for support. Robert and Sarah picked their way through crowds of street merchants heading for their shops, scholarly-looking young men dressed in black gowns sauntering to class, ragged-looking urchins begging or stealing a mouthful of bread, and fashionable men and women, hoping to be admired and envied, strolling along the narrow cobblestone paths. They were surprised at the number of French Huguenots, who wore their stark black and white attire with distinction. After asking several men for directions, they found the inn recommended to them by their fellow voyagers.

Hidden away in an alley off the Rue du Petit Moulton, the establishment had just five small rooms, a blessing for the couple fleeing from English authorities. The other occupants were two French clerks who had little interest in this English couple, a Flemish merchant, and a Scot whose occupation was unknown. Robert felt sure they were safe from discovery. In a few days Robert was ready to visit the home of a Monsieur Goudin, a textile merchant with young children in need of an English tutor.

"Sarah, promise me that when you go to the market that you will take care. Do not converse with any man or woman that you hear speaking English. Spies abound in all big cities."

"Mais oui, monsieur. J'obéirai a vos ordres." (Of course. I will obey your orders.)

"Parfait, ma cherie." (Perfect, my dear.)

Robert kissed her on both cheeks and smiled. Sarah had already learned some French and wanted him to know it. On board the boat, Robert had made a list of common French expressions that Sarah needed to know when she went to market. She learned these quickly, and within a few days, ventured out to explore this bustling city of merchants, potters, fishermen, printers, students, and the ever-present beggars.

When Robert arrived at the maison of Monsieur Goudin to apply for work as a tutor, the merchant was immediately impressed by Robert Pennyman's appearance. Goudin was a no-nonsense businessman, dark-eyed with a trimmed beard and smooth black hair who prided himself on his stylish dress. He wore a smart-looking outfit of high-quality cambric with silk lining, a shirt with a ruff at the collar, and silk hose. His boots were of the finest Spanish leather, and all his buttons were of gold. No tailor could have dressed a merchant better. The letters of recommendation from the textile merchants were effusive in praise of Robert's character. After asking Robert a series of pointed questions in French as well as English, a deal was struck. Goudin immediately offered him employment as the tutor of four of his five children, the youngest being but three years of age. Robert left there thinking that at least one problem was solved, a source of income. He knew that this was but the first step of his and Sarah's journey in a new life.

Sarah wrote once in code to her father to let him know that they had reached their destination safely. Given the capricious nature of the mail service, most likely it would not be in John Burton's hands for months. Life in Rouen was lively for some, but not for Sarah or Robert. They avoided making friends, talked to few people, and stayed as inconspicuous as possible. Sarah's weekly visits to the market were tedious because she could not engage in meaningful conversation except as it pertained to food purchases. Her pregnancy made her tire quickly, so, having much time on her hands, she read voraciously in both English and French. Robert had his work to relieve the boredom. Weeks and then months went by. What both of them prayed would never happen suddenly appeared one night.

Chapter Twenty-one

May 1608
Rouen, France
Danger

They were being followed. Robert was sure of it. He and Sarah were enjoying a dinner of fresh oysters, filet de Sandre Poele with potato, assorted cheeses, and a chocolate mousse. It was a meal that was not served anywhere in England, Robert told Sarah; even the king didn't dine so well. They were nearly finished when, as Robert lifted his glass to take a last sip of the sauvignon blanc, he found himself staring at a somewhat familiar face. Seated at a neighboring table was an unmistakable Englishman who was staring back at him. The man turned away, but Robert was sure he knew that visage. Dark eyes. Large nose. Pointed beard. It was an agent of the king! Robert had seen him at court. Zounds! What was he doing in Rouen? Robert caught Sarah's eye and through pursed lips said that they must leave the inn. He moved his fingers on the table to write a warning. Danger! Sarah nodded and neatly placed her napkin on the table. Then she stood up, and put on her linen cloak, lifting her hood to hide the telltale scar. Robert called for the proprietor in order to settle the bill. The owner slowly made his way over to their table, and Robert handed him several coins, waving him away. Then he and Sarah headed for the exit, which was in the opposite direction. The Englishman called to the owner as well, but it was a noisy, crowded room and the owner was heading for the kitchen. Robert and Sarah left the inn and started in the direction of the waterfront, away from their lodging. Their best chance of escape was diversion, but it also meant great danger for Sarah if Robert was captured or killed.

Robert considered his options. In Sarah's condition, five months pregnant, if they tried to run, they would not get far. He could attack and kill the king's hired man before he could alert anyone else, but Robert might be caught by the police or killed himself. What else could he do? His father had told him repeatedly that whenever a choice had to be made, there were never just two options but several. Most people saw only the most obvious, either this or that. There had to be another way. Even Sarah had alluded to this belief when she scolded Robert for not trying to talk to Essex's men when he encountered them. That time, he felt he had to either fight or flee. Now he decided to take Sarah's advice and confront the man to find out for sure why he was in Rouen.

At the first crossroads, Robert insisted that Sarah wend her way back to their inn by a circuitous route while he continued his casual stroll down to the docks. If she felt in any danger, she should use his dagger that he now placed in her hand.

"No, Robert, you may need this to save your life."

"I will think of some other way to avoid capture. You must be safe, and I have no doubt, that if need be, you will use the dagger to protect our unborn child."

She hesitated, not wanting to leave her husband, unarmed, at night in a foreign city with one of the king's men after him.

"Go! Now! While you still have the chance."

She turned to leave, but then stopped and looked at him with frightened, imploring eyes.

"You are in this difficulty because of me. I do not wish to have this baby without you beside me."

"Sarah, I cannot protect both of us. Have faith that I can escape."

He stepped away and moved as quickly as he dared toward the docks. Having no dagger hidden behind the back of his waist made him feel naked and vulnerable. He had only his wits to fend off an enemy. The agent in the inn certainly had seen him and Sarah leave, and if he was after Robert, he would quickly follow him. *Maybe*, Robert thought, *I will allow the king's agent to catch up and see what he does. If he tries to arrest me, I will heave him into the cold water, where the weight of his clothing will either drown him or delay him long enough for me to get away.*

There was a full moon out, so he was able to walk along the cobblestone streets easily. He was nearly at the waterfront when he heard footsteps behind him. He stopped and waited. Whoever it was continued to approach until Robert felt the man's warm breath on the back of his neck. He spun around, prepared for almost anything but what happened next. When he turned to confront his pursuer, the man smiled and held out his hand.

"Robert Dudley! It is you. I was not sure, for you are much changed." Robert had indeed tried to disguise his looks to avoid discovery; he was now clean-shaven and almost a stone heavier.

"Charles Percy, is it not? What brings you to Rouen?" Robert tried to speak calmly, but his voice trembled a little.

"The king heard rumors of a Catholic plot and asked me to track them down. I have only just arrived. What are you doing here, besides enjoying the company of French women?"

Robert smiled broadly, more from relief than from pleasure.

"I needed to get away from England. I could not shake the memories of my beloved Anne whose untimely death caused me much grief."

"Ah, yes. As I remember, she was sought after by an elderly lord to whom the king owed a favor, but she refused him and still the king did not permit you to marry her. I suppose it was just as well, her being so sickly." Robert simply nodded. He wanted to get Charles to change the subject.

"Are you staying in Rouen long?"

"Alas, no. My mission is to travel on to Paris and meet an informant. I expect to be there awhile."

A strong breeze was coming off the Seine River, and both men wrapped their cloaks around them tightly. Robert was anxious to get back to Sarah so he kept silent, hoping that this unwelcome Englishman would just leave.

Charles broke the silence.

"I am staying at an inn near where we had supper. Shall we walk back together and share a bottle of wine? The burgundy is quite good." Robert shook his head.

"Not tonight. I am heading to a small lodging along the water to meet a woman."

"I am a poor substitute for a lady of the evening. Good luck to you."

They shook hands and went off in opposite directions. As soon as Charles was out of sight, Robert doubled back to where he had left Sarah and followed along the route that he had asked her to take. He raced back all the way to their inn, praying for her safety. He found Sarah pacing the floor with worry. She fell into his arms.

"Robert, thank God you are back. Are you all right? What happened?"

"It was indeed one of the king's agents, but he was not looking for me, but English Catholics who want to overthrow the king and return our country to Catholicism. Thankfully, he is not staying here but continuing on to Paris. But when he gets back to England, he will surely find out that I am being hunted and tell King James of my being here. Rouen is not as safe as I imagined. We must be prepared to leave this city as soon as our child is born."

Chapter Twenty-two

May 1608
Rouen, France
New Plans

"Where shall we go? The king has spies everywhere in Europe. Where can we hide that is safe?" Sarah rubbed her abdomen, swollen with child, as she spoke. What kind of life would their infant be born into, if they had to be constantly fleeing from King James's wrath?

Robert looked at her with alarm. Had he foolishly insisted they leave England for France, only to leave France for some other foreign country? He could always earn a living in France, being able to speak the language and perhaps in Spain as well, but he had no connections in that country and getting there would be long and expensive. In other European countries, he would be at an extreme disadvantage because he was not fluent in other tongues. He was willing to take chances, but not to the point of making him and his family destitute.

"I will think of something," he said, realizing how empty and vague those words sounded.

That night they both slept the sleep of tortured souls, waking at every sound and getting small comfort from being enveloped in the warmth of their entwined bodies. When morning came, they went about their routines like prisoners about to be executed. They ate little, spoke less, and kept their eyes on the tasks at hand.

The next day, Robert left early for the home of his employer, hoping that a long walk would clear his mind and give him an answer to the question pounding in his brain—where to go next? He was deep in thought when, passing by a group of French Huguenots with their characteristic black-and-white attire, he heard one say, "*Mon cousin est arrive a Liverpool et est en securite.*" (My cousin has arrived in Liverpool and is safe.) Robert felt as if his head had just exploded. Of course! That was what he and Sarah must do. They could go back to England and hide in a coastal town where strangers were coming and going constantly. He and Sarah would be accepted as English folk and the king would not think of looking for them back in England, especially when he found out that they have been seen in France. He could not wait to get back to the apartment that night to tell Sarah.

It was Sarah's day to visit the marketplace, but she was not eager to go. Being noticeably pregnant increased her prominence among the merchants and customers. A woman, pregnant and alone in a public square, was full of danger. She might be thought a prostitute or a beggar who would do anything for a sou. Robert had asked her to wait until he was home before venturing out, but Sarah had convinced him that she could use her wits, just as he did, to get out of any difficult situation. She wanted to be strong and independent and felt she had something to prove.

She left in mid-afternoon, hoping that the market would be less crowded and so allowing her to shop easily. As she made her way down the narrow, cobblestone street toward the square, she heard a voice behind her say, "*Mademeoiselle, vondriez-vous mes merchandises?*" (Do you want to see my merchandise?) Sarah turned to see a man in rags glaring at her and pointing to his midsection. He stared at her scar and gave a triumphant smile, imagining he had found a battered woman, willing to have sex for little or no money. She thought it best to continue to the market without speaking to him, but he continued to follow her closely, keeping up an obnoxious chatter. She looked around for someone who might help her. There was a cluster of young men in high spirits heading home from the university; she doubted that they would feel chivalrous toward her. The odds were better if she depended on her wits to escape from this disgusting pig. She quickened her pace, but the dogged man easily kept up. The market was still a distance away, down one long narrow street and then across an open square to another. She could smell the stench of the man's unwashed body. There was nowhere to run or hide; in fact, the three-storied lopsided structures ran the length of both sides of the street, drooping upon each other like tired bodies, not letting in a crack of sunlight but creating dark areas that gave cover to illegal behavior.

She thought of the miracle of her getting pregnant, and of her need to protect her unborn child. She was determined not to let this creature have his way with her. The memories of the encounter with the intruder in her home years ago were still vivid. If this man as much as touched her, she would—. She suddenly felt his hand grabbing at her arm. No! It would not happen again. She whirled around and smashed her fist against his face so hard, she heard a crack. The man fell backward, and she took off in spite of her enlarged belly, lifting up her dress so as not to trip. When she reached the corner, she stopped and pressed herself against the side of the building, gasping for breath. Her chest was heaving, her cheeks were flushed, and beads of sweat fell down her face, blocking out her vision. She put her hands on her abdomen, holding the swelling as if to protect its contents. Her fist was red and sore, proof of how hard she had hit her attacker. She secretly hoped that she had broken his nose.

There was no way she could continue to the market, so circling around the block, she made her way back to the inn, looking behind her every few steps. The passageway up to their room looked darker and steeper than what she remembered. Every creak of the stairs and every shadow in a corner terrified her. Her hand throbbed, and her back ached. Her body was shaking from fear and exertion. When she tried to put the key in the lock, it fell to the floor with such a clatter that she screamed and immediately put her hand over her mouth to stifle the sound.

Finally, the key went in and Sarah stumbled into the room, shivering in spite of the heat. She collapsed on top of the bedcovers and started to sob, tears for what she had to endure here in Rouen and more tears for that violent attack on her person years ago. She cried for herself and for all women who had to suffer such indignities and assaults. She cried for her babe in her womb and the world that it would come to know that allowed such behavior. She cried until her throat burned and her lungs ached. Finally, she fell into a sleep so deep that when Robert arrived home and saw her on the bed fully dressed, he tried to wake her but could not. Telling her about his idea to return to England would have to wait until later.

It was nearly dark when Sarah rose from their bed, still shaken and hurting from the punch she had launched at her assailant. Robert's immediate reaction on hearing of the assault was to find the bastard and kill him. Sarah told him he was not thinking logically. There was no way to track down the man who assaulted her. Then he began to blame Sarah for not being more careful. His tirade of reprimands and criticism made Sarah cringe.

"I warned you not to go out alone," he yelled. "Why didn't you obey me and wait until I came home?"

"Stop it, Robert," Sarah said quietly. "You are my husband, not my master. You must respect my wits."

"I can't respect your wits when you act so foolishly."

"I am a grown woman. I cannot love you if you treat me like a child. If you ever scold me again, I will leave you and go back to the Mews to live my life as I wish."

Robert stared in disbelief.

"You don't mean that," he replied.

"Do you doubt me? Because if you do, I will pack my things right now and find a boat back to England." Robert's head sagged, and he sat in the nearest chair and thought of the implications of what his wife was telling him. He remembered how Sarah behaved when he first came to the Mews after he had berated her for knowing so much. It would do no good to be cross with her. He felt ashamed that he had lost his temper and had no doubt that his wife would do just as she threatened she would.

"I only wanted to let you know how much your safety means to me," he said softly. "We must leave here at once and find a place to stay in a quiet neighborhood, away from such debauchers."

He took her in his arms and held her tight. He promised himself never to lose his temper again. She was his whole world.

"Yes," she agreed. "Perhaps your employer will help us to find other lodgings."

Robert had made a commitment to teach Monsieur Goudin's children, and he wanted to remain at that post until a few months after the baby arrived when their child and Sarah were fit to travel. The next day Robert explained his situation to the merchant but, no sooner had he spoken the words, when Goudin offered his own home as a refuge.

"Your wife must be safe. Bring her here. We have room for you both, and my wife has much experience in birthing." When Robert tried to protest, his employer would not hear of it.

"*Elle va rester ici. Fini.*" (She will stay here. Done.)

Marie Goudin was a stocky woman with large, round eyes, pointed nose, and double chin. Her favorite expression was *"Sacre bleu"* whenever something went wrong. With five children, that happened frequently. The children asked Sarah so many questions and corrected her French so often that she was beginning to think in French first when she was queried about something. The isolation of their tiny apartment was soon forgotten, and she basked in the games and silliness that all children relish. It was good preparation for motherhood.

Although Monsieur Goudin tried to persuade the couple to remain with them after the birth or to at least live nearby, Robert told his employer that he and Sarah decided to find a home in a small town somewhere along the southwest coast of England. Sarah had been ecstatic when Robert told her of his idea. Although there was so much about France that she loved—the food, the weather, the culture, the language with its curious idioms—she missed her father dearly and was worried that he would become depressed to have to live out his life without his only child to comfort him. And what a joy it would be for him to see his grandchild. The Mews was only forty miles from the coast, one hard day's journey by horseback. Her father could visit them often, pretending that he was traveling to meet other learned men. His servant Jack could be trusted to keep the real purpose secret. *Oh, so many secrets,* Sarah thought. Her marrying Robert, hiding from the king, Robert pretending to be a yeoman and she a servant. *Did other people have to live this way?* she wondered. She thought about something Mary Sidney, the Countess of Pembroke, had said to her when advising her to flee with Robert. "You must keep your lives in hugger-mugger as we all do; you cannot trust the air with secrets." She wondered what secrets Mary Sidney was hiding.

Chapter Twenty-three

August 1608
Rouen, France
Birth and Rebirth

Robert and Sarah's child was born nine months to the day that they had made love in the bedroom at his parents' manor. That act had produced more than a child; it created a terror. Their daughter was born with spit and fire in her blood. She wailed when she was hungry and grabbed fingers, noses, and whatever else was in her reach and wouldn't let go until someone pried loose her tentacles. She gurgled when she was tickled or sung to, and slept not nearly enough for her parents' liking. Monsieur Goudin's children made it their mission to see which of them drew the most laughter from her chest and fought to see who could hold her the longest. For Sarah, it was like having a bevy of performers and babysitters at the ready. The couple agonized over what to name her and finally decided on two names—Mary after Sarah's mother and Elizabeth after Robert's sister. But she was never referred to as Mary Elizabeth. She was forever called Lizzie, and it suited her looks and personality perfectly. Her hair was red and frizzy, her lively eyes green with flecks of yellow, and her skin was rosy. She was the epitome of a child-turned-firecracker. Whenever she was awake, she made noises, and as soon as she was given any toy, she tasted it, squeezed it, and, determining it was of no interest, dropped it on the floor. Invariably, anyone who was close by picked it up and put it in her hand and the scene repeated itself. The babbles that came out of her mouth were more like insistent demands to be heeded. Here was a child one could not ignore.

Three months later, Robert and Sarah prepared for the journey back to England. Robert had made inquiries with a friend who had a cousin living in the coastal backwater town of Netley, which was of no consequence to the king. However, it was close to Southampton, which was a hub of activity due to the number of ships sailing from there to mainland countries of Europe, especially France and Spain. Besides sailors, longshoremen, and suppliers, there were wainwrights, merchants, innkeepers, custom house clerks, and tutors to the children of wealthy businessmen. If Robert found employment in Southampton, their child had a chance to live a normal life in England. If danger did appear, they were close to the sea and an escape route.

It was Sarah who thought of a possible occupation, that of a scrivener.

"If you hire yourself out to copy documents for merchants, you can stay well hidden behind closed doors."

It was not at all suited to Robert's abilities and interests, but he thought it was necessary while he explored other avenues of income more in keeping with his education and background. Deep down he knew that there was little likelihood of an important position. In England, as in all of Europe, a man's future lay in his past. The house he was born into, the ancestors he had, and the occupation of his father determined his future. Now that Robert had severed all connections with his past, who or what was he? The reality of his present situation made him edgy and morose.

The voyage back to England was more terrifying than the voyage to France. It was early spring, with gray and blustery skies, which mirrored their mood. Sarah worried about what lay ahead for Lizzie, while Robert brooded over what lay ahead for them all. Lizzie attracted unwanted attention with her antics, and Sarah kept her below decks as much as possible. The baby enjoyed the rocking of the boat and slept a great deal more than usual. Finally, the sight of the English coastline came into view and raised their spirits.

They disembarked in Southampton and immediately took a carriage to the address of his friend's cousin who was to advise them about employment and lodging. John Beecham was a trader of woolen textiles to France. He knew where money was to be made and spoke proudly of his accomplishments.

"Get yourself in with the merchants who supply ships, and you will have yourself a good situation. I will introduce you to a few."

"Yes, that is good advice. Remember to call me Robert Pennyman to anyone we meet."

"Yes, of course. There is a sea captain's widow who rents rooms in her large house. She will have no problem taking in such a respectable couple as you two, but mind you, there are spies and unsavory characters about who would turn you in for a six pence. Trust no one, and you will have safety here."

The widow's house in the village of Netley was a two-chimneyed, half-timbered building overlooking the entrance to Southampton Harbor. It was built on a knoll above salt marshes and had grand views of the conflux between the Test and Itchen rivers. The couple rented three rooms on the second floor that were connected to each other by doors. The glazed windows overlooked the entire expanse of the shore and the rivers beyond. It was such a delightful view that Sarah spent every free minute watching the activity on the water and secretly hoped that someday she and Robert could afford such a grand house.

The first morning, the couple and the baby came down to eat a breakfast that the widow had prepared. Then Robert borrowed the landlady's horse and rode the short distance to Southampton to inquire after employment. He and John Beecham walked around the dock and stopped at the maritime offices of several merchants, but scriveners were not needed by them. Robert was becoming anxious. He needed to find employment quickly. Beecham suggested that they try a new business that had just opened up. There the merchant said he had a position for just such work, but Beecham introduced his friend as Robert Dudley and quickly realized his mistake. There was no way to correct it and Robert felt compelled to accept the job without using an alias.

At their new home, Sarah washed or ironed or sewed while Lizzie played on the floor with a spinning top, and a stuffed doll that Sarah made out of cloth scraps and buttons. Then mother and daughter left the house to go along the paths leading down to the shore. The widow had a well-used cart, fashioned from two small wheels, an iron rod, and a wooden box; it had been used to bring her husband's belongings on board his ship. With Lizzie stuffed inside it, and ropes tied across the opening to keep her secure, Sarah pulled the cart along the gravel walks and rocky shore where sea birds swooped and fish splashed.

The port was full of watercraft of all kind, from rowboats to barques to galleons. Some ships left the harbor gliding under half sail, and fishing boats returned laden down with their catch. She heard the distant cries of men shouting and marveled as the waves pounded against the sides of the barques. She had never seen such activity as this, never at the Mews which was far from the sea and hardly ever in Rouen, since while there, she had kept hidden in her chambers. Now she breathed in the salty air and let the wind blow against her cloak. Ever since her marriage to Robert, she had lived in hiding. Here she felt truly free from fear and free from confinement.

As for Robert, when he returned home in the evenings from the merchant's office, his delight in Lizzie's antics knew no bounds. She tugged at his beard, newly grown, and giggled when he roared in imagined pain. She mussed his hair, grabbed his legs, and begged to be picked up. He, in turn, pretended to be a clown juggling balls or a monster lurching with clawed fingers or a duck waddling toward her. Sarah watched with pleasure, only wishing that her father was there to see how his daughter's life had progressed.

Chapter Twenty-four

Summer 1610
Southampton, England

Death Comes to Town

Lizzie was two years old when the plague descended on England, suffocating nearly every city and town with its invisible cloud of disease. It invaded magnificent mansions and humble hovels with equal ferocity, ravaging the population, irregardless of age, social standing, or piety. Sarah kept her only child indoors as much as possible to avoid contact with others, but then the sea captain's wife came to collect the rent and stayed to reminisce about her own dead children. The woodsman came with logs for the fireplace and took out his knife to carve a wooden trinket for her daughter, musicians appeared on the road with drums and flutes, the sounds of which lured every child outdoors, neighbors dropped by with delectable treats just for Lizzie. Sarah wanted the world to disappear, but instead, it came right to her doorstep.

Church attendance was compulsory on Sundays, and the local bishop enforced the law, even in times of plague, not wanting to lose one pence in contributions to the Lord God. The folk who came to church, whether religious or indifferent about the Creator, might either spread the contagion or be infected with it. On Sundays Robert and Sarah looked at the increasing number of empty pews and wondered which was the greater peril: attending church and coming into contact with the disease, or staying in the safety of their home and being reviled by the church minister for missing Sunday service and made to pay a fine of 15 shillings for each infraction. He had already spent the small purse that his father begrudgingly had given him. The money that Robert earned at his employment had to go a long way to cover their expenses, and there would be no further inheritance from his father.

When market day arrived, Sarah was forced to bring Lizzie along since she had no one else to mind her. The healthy, the sick who could still walk, and the maids who treated those afflicted also came to the town square to buy food. It was not the happy occasion as it was in the past; no one wanted to greet neighbors and exchange gossip. No matter how much she tried, Sarah and her daughter could not escape being in close contact with carriers of the pestilence. Oh, how Sarah wished for her mother, long since dead from complications in childbirth or for her father, who still did not know that Sarah was only forty miles away. She had begged Robert to allow her to send him a letter in code, letting him know their new whereabouts, but Robert had convinced her that this was not the time to chance a letter, even a coded one, since the place of origin might be found out. He suggested that they wait a while to be sure they were safe from suspicion. But to Sarah, it was cruel.

In the end, the plague came to the neighborhoods of Dr. John Burton and Robert and Sarah Dudley. A rural farmer bringing butter and cheese for export reported to the offices where Robert worked.

"I have just come from Wells and have found the countryside sickened with disease. There is hardly a cottage that is not infected. Bodies lay covered on the ground with no able men to bury them."

Robert overheard this, and he took the sad news back to Sarah who cursed herself for not going to see her father who had sacrificed so much for her and Robert's happiness. She told Robert that she was going to the Mews to visit him, with or without his consent. She packed that night, ignoring Lizzie who was unusually fussy.

The next morning Lizzie took ill with fever, developed black lumps on her groin, and cried constantly for water. Robert was away at work and could escape Lizzie's discomfort, but Sarah's heart broke as she watched her miracle child in such pain. Holding Lizzie in her arms had no effect in trying to comfort her. Day after day, the two year old grew weaker and her fever did not abate. Robert's reaction on seeing Lizzie so sickly was to leave the house because he did not want to hear her moans. He began to spend longer hours at work and then went to taverns, hoping that his daughter would be asleep when he returned home. In desperation, Sarah decided to take Lizzie to the Mews to see her father. She felt an urgency about it, fearing that if she did not go now, she would surely never see him again. It was absurd for her to think that he could save Lizzie, but she had to let him see her. Sitting at home, waiting for Lizzie to die was like having an archer shoot arrows at her until one pierced her heart and killed her. At the very least, she hoped to see her aging father alive and that he could take joy and comfort in her presence. She, as his only living relative, owed him that.

Horseback was the fastest way to cover the forty miles from Southampton to the Mews so Sarah borrowed the landlady's old mount, and flew over the ground with Lizzie strapped around her waist like a girdle. She had not received Robert's blessing, but he knew better than to try to force Sarah to do anything that she did not want to do. Robert reasoned that both mother and daughter were heading into a noxious swamp of filth and corrupt air. He did not want to lose both of them in a foolish, desperate journey, but he could not stop them nor could he join them. His income was what was feeding them, and if he suddenly left for God knows how long, his employer would surely fire him.

Sarah left very early the next morning, just as the sky was beginning to change from inky black to a smoky gray. A woman traveling alone was most in danger at night so she determined that if they stopped just once around noon, she would arrive at the Mews by dusk. The horse's rocking motion put Lizzie to sleep, and for that, Sarah was grateful. The ground was sun baked and hard, which made the horse move with speed and vigor, like it, too, was on a mission of importance.

By noon, they had reached Salisbury and Sarah stopped at a small inn on the outskirts, wishing to avoid coming across anyone from the Dudley household. She and Lizzie dismounted, and the horse was taken into the stable to be fed and rested, but it was doubtful that she could continue on to the Mews with the same horse. It was old and looked weary.

Inside the inn, the owner's wife, when asked for some broth for the *young feverish child, said, "I have just the thing to make her better." She* left and returned shortly with a bowl of something she called "magic soup." "I give it to all my guests who are feeling poorly and they are made right again, quick as a wink." Sarah demanded to know what was in it. The woman looked as if she could be a witch with her hair all ragged edged and her clothes as coarse as a rasp. However, the color on her cheeks and the spark in her eyes showed that she was hale and hearty.

"I make it mostly from vegetables and spices and, of course, molasses. That makes it tasty. But it is my secret ingredient that cures what ails ye, ain't that so, Bess?" The woman sitting nearby nodded vigorously. Sarah, who was in no condition to argue, watched while the woman spooned the drink into her daughter's mouth. Sarah took some of the nourishment herself, and it was at least palatable. She kept an eye on Lizzie to see how the concoction affected her. There was no change. The fever still raged.

Sarah dared to stay there for only an hour. She had to get a fresh horse and made her way over to the stable. It was an expense she cursed, but it had to be paid if she expected to reach the Mews by nightfall. She promised to return it in a few days and to take her landlady's horse back. A fresh steed was provided, and after twenty miles, the tiny hamlet of Mere appeared. She looked for signs that the plague had been there and found them. The doors of some cottages were boarded up. Fresh graves dug. No one was outside enjoying the mild summer twilight. Even the stables seemed empty. She slowed her horse to a trot and, fearing the worst, approached the door of her former home. It was dark with only a dim light flickering through the window in the parlor. At least, someone was home. She hoped, she prayed that it was her father, as healthy as any seventy year old man could be. She dismounted with Lizzie still strapped around her like a security belt, keeping her from harm. Now only the door stood between her and the occupant inside. Her hand grasped the knocker, and she rapped lightly. No one stirred. Gathering up her courage, she began to pound and called out, "Father, it is me, Sarah. Open the door."

Someone came running around the corner from the stable. It was Peter, who stopped in his tracks when he saw her. He rubbed his eyes in disbelief.

"Peter, it is me, Sarah." She motioned for him to take the reins of the horse and was about to ask him about her father when a sound was heard within. The wooden bar was lifted and the door opened just a crack. Two eyes peered into the darkness outside. Then with flourish, the door flashed open and Jane cried out, "Miss Sarah, you've come back."

Sarah was just as surprised to see Jane for she hardly ever remained at the Mews at night.

"What has happened, Jane? Where is my father?"

"He lies in bed, ill with fever and chills. I am nursing him as best I can."

"Take me to him!"

Jane saw movement under Sarah's cloak and a mop of red curls came into view, followed by a pair of green eyes, a small nose, and red lips. Finally, Lizzie's rosy cheeks appeared and a soft whimper was heard, like a hungry kitten looking for milk.

"What…is this," Jane blurted out, and immediately wished she could retract her words for she suddenly realized that the apparition materializing from the depths of black woolen fabric had to be Sarah's daughter.

Sarah undid the binding that had held Lizzie firmly in place and produced a complete girl. "This is my Lizzie, and I believe she is thirsty. Is there any goat's milk for her?"

"Why, yes. I milked the goats a short while ago and gave a cup to your father. I will fetch a cup for your little girl." She smiled at Lizzie who clung to her mother, looking wide-eyed and frightened. Sarah whispered words of comfort, and pushed Lizzie's hair away from her face. In doing so, she touched Lizzie's forehead and was surprised at how cool it felt. Maybe it was just because Lizzie had been outside for so long, she reasoned. Then she looked at Lizzie's eyes. They were less glassy than in the morning. Both were signs that the fever and chills from yesterday were less severe. Jane returned with a mug of warm milk, and Lizzie drank it all.

"More, Mamma. More milk, please."

"God be praised!" Sarah cried. "God be praised." She started to remove Lizzie's clothes to check to see if the lumps on her groin were gone, but she was stopped by a faraway sound. A deep voice floated down the staircase, making everyone turn to look as if the sound and the body that produced it were inseparable. "Who is there, Jane?" came the unmistakable words of John Burton.

"Father, it is me." Sarah moved to the staircase, with Lizzie hanging onto her hip. Clutching the railing, her legs still bent and stiff from the long ride, she moved up the stairs like a bow-legged sailor climbing up to the crow's nest. The upstairs hall led into four bedchambers and her father's was at the far end. Each step she took was both fearful and joyful. Looking down at Lizzie, now wide awake and temporarily full, Sarah whispered, "We are going to see Grandfather."

"Granfa?"

Her daughter's saying that word brought tears to her eyes and pain to her heart. *How could I have left him for so long without letting him meet his only grandchild?* she thought. Some risks were worth taking, and this one was surely a necessary gamble. Her father, living alone for nearly three years and now sick, was probably much changed, and Sarah braced herself for the transformation. His room was much as it had been: a wide bed with curtained hangings, a small side table on which sat a glowing candle, a pair of spectacles, and a glass half filled with milk, an oak chair like the one downstairs by the fireplace, and a chest filled with clothes. Her father's face was half hidden behind a gauzy curtain, but through it she could see his shock of white hair, looking longer and more untidy than it had ever been, and it made her tremble.

"Father, I have returned."

She and Lizzie, as one, moved to his bedside.

"Who is it?" he said, staring first at Sarah and then at Lizzie. Sarah realized that her father did not have his spectacles on, so she reached over, picked them up, and placed them in his shaky hands. He put them on, looked at the two figures before him, and started to cry.

"You have come back," he repeated over and over again while trying to hug them both at once. He squeezed them so hard that Lizzie, who was buried in his embrace, squealed to be free.

Her father insisted she tell the whole story then and there, even though she could see him tiring. It took a while for Sarah to explain what had happened in the years since she and Robert had fled the Mews.

When she finished, she was very tired herself.

"We will speak again in the morning. Good night, dear Father. You need to rest."

"Now that you and my granddaughter are here, I feel new strength. Good night, little one. Your being here shall make me well."

Dr. Burton's condition did improve, but it was only temporary. His illness had weakened his heart and lungs. Within a few days his coughing increased and he wheezed constantly. Sarah decided to stay with him to the end and asked Jane to find someone to deliver a letter to Robert, but with so many folks sick or caring for someone, there was no one to be found.

When a week passed and he had received no word from Sarah, Robert took to drinking at pubs before venturing home to an empty apartment and he often got into scrapes with the rugged men who came off the ships looking for some roughhousing. He dismissed Sarah's warning that he needed to stay hidden. He no longer cared about his safety. He concluded that with Sarah and Lizzie heading into mortal danger, there was little chance that they would return to him. No one was left that he loved or who loved him. One night he sat alone at a bar while sailors whooped it up around him. They finally took notice of him and his occupation as a scrivener.

"Looky here, mates. This gent has black fingernails. Must be hard work pickin' up a quill and pushin' it across a paper."

Laughter spread around the pub from men who had just spent the better part of a year swabbing decks and unfurling sails.

Robert looked up from his tankard of ale with fire in his eyes. What had his life become, he thought. An object for ignorant jack tars to toy with? He stood up and faced his tormentors.

"I challenge you to a fight, you whoring, thieving sea dogs. With my hands, I'll tear you apart."

The sailor, figuring that he had chosen a timid clerk to pick on, was surprised by Robert's violent response.

"Just teasin', mate. No need for fisticuffs."

This time a fight was averted, but Robert was becoming lax in his promise to Sarah to always be on guard. All that was needed was one person to recognize him and the jig was up.

One week later, Dr. Burton died. Sarah remained at the Mews just long enough to bury him in the family cemetery beside his wife. Then she quickly closed up the house, said her sad goodbyes to Jane and Peter, and mother and daughter returned to Southampton, to an overjoyed and grateful husband. Robert was deeply saddened by the news of his father-in-law's death. John Burton had supported him and Sarah all through their stay at the Mews and had helped them with disguises and letters of commerce to reach the coast safely.

"I am glad you went to see him, Sarah. It was not right for me to try to prevent you. It was my own selfishness. I love you both so much and do not want any harm to come to you or to Lizzie."

BOOK THREE

Mary Sidney and her son William Herbert

Chapter One

Fall 1610

London

A Visit of Some Consequence

On a gray autumn morning, a humble carriage approached the entrance to the London home of Lord William Herbert and his wife, Mary Talbot. At the steps leading up to the imposing entrance, it stopped and out came a man of no real importance. He was merely an actor and a part owner of a theatre company and, as such, hardly merited a grand welcome. His attire was a mixture of colors and fabrics in a foolhardy attempt to impress his host, but it only revealed his humble heritage. His red velvet waistcoat was worn and out of date, his brown leather breeches, plain and baggy, did not complement his bright green jacket and yellowed silk hose, all of which looked strung together like a harlequin's costume.

He was made to wait in the expansive hall, while the lord of the house was informed of his arrival. Then a servant escorted him down a long corridor to one of the smaller sitting rooms. Lord William Herbert, in a handsome doublet of green velvet and matching breeches, was standing next to a great oak desk on which lay piles of vellum paper, several fine goose quills, and a bottle of black ink. His head was bent toward the windows, as he tried to read from a paper he held away from his body.

His wig lay on a side table, apparently not needed to impress today's visitor. His exposed pate revealed a thinning of his curly red hair at the top of his head and around his temples, which made his large nose all the more prominent. The visitor was announced and crept in, not wishing to disturb his lordship. He stood in the doorway and bowed very low. His lordship kept on reading. Finally, without waiting for his host to speak first, the visitor blurted out, "Good morrow, M'Lord. I was delighted by your accepting my request to visit you and may I say that you are looking exceedingly well."

Lord William looked up in surprise. His pudgy belly and flushed face belied a common habit of overindulging in rich food and fine wines. He cast a withering glance at the figure's attire and snickered.

"Good morrow, Master Shakespeare. It has been several years since we last spoke. How does your theatre company fare in this time of plague?"

"My Lord, the Globe has remained opened due to your influence with the king, and we are performing a play nearly every day. My humble thanks." Again he bowed very low.

"That is most commendable. What play is being performed now?"

"*Cymbeline*, M'Lord. It is much loved by the audiences, especially the characters of Jachimo and Postumus. But I am here to speak to you on a most urgent matter. The printer Thorpe has published a volume of sonnets under my name. This has caused me great embarrassment because many of them are written to a young man and express ardor towards him. Consider the several sonnets about loving a sweet boy. Several others ask a man to wed and have children. I urge you to have them retracted."

"That cannot be done. It is unfortunate that such an inference is made. However, the sonnets are very popular and worthy of publication."

"M'Lord, then I beg you to use your influence to stop further copies from publication. Consider my reputation."

William had no concerns for the actor's reputation since there were many rumors of the actor frequenting an inn where he reportedly was on intimate terms with the innkeeper's wife. Unfortunately, circumstances were such that the lord needed to appease this man who was a writer in name only.

"Very well. I will order the printer to publish no more editions for now."

"My most humble thanks, my gracious lord. You have been most kind and generous to me in the past and I continue to be most discreet in all the matters which we have discussed."

"My generosity comes with conditions, as you well know. As a beard, you must never reveal the source of these works. If you do, I will deny everything you say and have you thrown in prison. I understand that you have bought some property for a considerable amount of cash. Several hundred pounds, in fact. Pray that nobody asks where that money came from. Your profession as an actor does not pay well enough, nor does your part-ownership of a theatre."

"Yes, M'Lord. I mean, no, M'Lord, it comes from your purse and for that I most grateful. Does your, that is, do you have another play for me?"

William gave the man a stern look. "I have one here before me. The title is *The Winter's Tale* based on a novel by Robert Greene."

The visitor looked angry.

"What is the matter?"

"Nothing, M'Lord. Tis only that Greene accused me of stealing the works of other poets."

"You would do well to keep your temper. It can only draw suspicion to these writings. Take them and be on your way. That will be all. Good day to you."

"And to you, M'Lord." The man again bowed low and, stuffing the papers in his pocket, scurried out of the room.

William had not asked his mother for permission to print the sonnets. She had already left to spend the winter on the Continent, but he knew that when she heard of it, she would be enraged. There were several sonnets that were very personal to her, especially the ones she wrote to his uncle Philip, begging him to marry and produce heirs. His mother had been very close to her older brother; in fact, she claimed that they had been of one mind on a great many matters, especially poetry, each encouraging the other to write verses and collaborating to write the *Psalms of David*. His memory of his uncle was blurry as he was only five years old when Philip died, but he recalled his mother was inconsolable with grief upon hearing of his death. He remembered her drawn face, her cries of anguish, and her kneeling in prayer, paying little attention to him or his siblings for weeks and months on end. It took two whole years for her to get over her brother's death and become a mother again.

Now she had another reason to be unhappy. So be it, he thought. Just another injury that she would add to her account of his failings. Another abomination of his character. They had not spoken since 1604, six years since he first accused her of having an affair with Lister and six years since he realized that it was she who was writing plays as well as sonnets. She knew very well that these works could never be published in her name; she had decided on her own that the actor Shakespeare would do as a beard although he had few credentials to warrant the protection of such a large and commendable body of work.

And then there was the whole affair with Anne, planning for her demise so she did not have to marry a nobleman chosen by the Crown. How devious and diabolic his mother had become. There was so much more to his mother than he had ever imagined or wanted to know. She had recently taken up residence with Dr. Lister at Crosby Hall in London, living with him openly as if being a dowager countess was not enough status to see her through her old age. He thanked God that she was out of Wilton House for good. Whatever mischief was afoot with her, she must deal with on her own.

Chapter Two

Spring 1611
Crosby Hall, London
A Thankless Child

"He knew…he knew the sonnets were my expression of unhappiness about an unmarried brother and my anguish over his too soon death. Why did William have them printed when he knew they were only for my eyes and those in my favor?"

Mary paced up and down the ornate sitting room at Crosby Hall as Matthew Lister sat reading a book of sonnets with William Shakespeare listed as the author.

"How can William expect Shakespeare to claim ownership to sonnets that were written to urge my brother to marry and to father babes who will carry his image and virtues forever forward? Who would believe it? William has committed the cruelest cut of all—betrayal to a mother who has protected and defended him before the Crown when he was unworthy of such aid."

Matthew raised his head and said softly, "Mary, the deed is done. Perhaps William felt this was the only way to preserve the verses."

"That is cold comfort."

"I doubt that Shakespeare would deny ownership, even though many of them seem strange to be written by a man. Shakespeare, having claimed ownership to some, must know own them all."

"And so I am left without recourse or without hope that this can ever be righted."

"Mary, you cannot change the world by yourself. Do not allow your bile to rule you. Do you remember when you were very angry with me because you thought I was having an affair with your young cousin? You became very despondent and bitter. It did not become you then, and it does not become you now."

"Ah, yes. I took my anger out with my pen and wrote sonnets to my cousin about it.

> So, now I have confessed that he is thine,
> And I myself am mortgaged to thy will,
> Myself I'll forfeit so that other mine
> Thou wilt restore, to be my comfort still;
> But thou wilt not, nor he will not be free,
> For thou art covetous, and he is kind;

You are indeed kind, kinder than I sometimes deserve."

Matthew looked at Mary with sympathetic eyes.

"You alone have the power to decide your humor." He looked down at the open book he was still holding and turned the page.

"Here, in this one sonnet, you change from despair to hope."

"Read it to me, Matthew."

> "When in disgrace with fortune and men's eyes,
> I all alone beweep my outcast state,
> And trouble deaf heaven with my bootless cries

> And look upon myself, and curse my fate,
>
> Wishing me like to one more rich in hope'
>
> Featured like him, like him with friends possest,
>
> Desiring this man's art and that man's scope,
>
> With what I most enjoy contented least;"

Mary broke in and continued:

> "Yet in these thoughts myself almost despising,
>
> Haply I think of thee, —and then my state,
>
> Like to the lark at break of day arising
>
> From sullen earth, sings hymns at heaven's gate;
>
> For thy sweet love remembered such wealth brings,
>
> That then I scorn to change my state with kings.

That is still how I feel when you are with me, my dear Matthew. My heart makes my fingers write such verse."

"Mary, you have been able to publish so much in your own name: *Antonius, Discourse of Life and Death, Arcadia, the Psalms of David, Astrea,* and others. There are few women, if any, who can claim such achievements."

"Matthew, you can always make my despair turn against itself. Forgive me if I am too much preoccupied with wanting justice. I am selfish. No more talk of this. I will continue to write what I please and pray that it will be read by the public and delight audiences in the theaters."

"Yes, and times may change. Find a way to preserve them in your name, secret them away, and future generations may acclaim your greatness."

"My sweet Matthew, I am blessed to have you with me."

"I am yours 'til death do us part."

"A way to preserve them in my name. Yes, that is it. I must devise something like my musical code. Sir Francis Bacon described a code he invented using only the letters "a" and "b". Each letter of the alphabet was represented by a five letter series of "a" and "b". Of course, I don't have to use those two letters. I could use any two I choose, like "m" and "s", my initials. You have given me inspiration. I will get started on it directly."

Chapter Three

Summer 1614
Spa, Belgium
Get Thee a Good Husband

"I do love you, dearer than sight, space, or liberty."

Mary kissed Matthew full on the lips as they sat, side by side, on the gold damasked sofa in their sitting room at their residence in Spa. She delighted in his warm embrace and caressing touch. There was no need to hide their love here in Belgium. Having her lover with her while she vacationed away from prying eyes and accusing lips was the freedom and privilege that she had sought for so many years, since Matthew Lister first came to Wilton House, as the resident doctor. Ten years younger than herself and possessing the intelligence, manners, and grace of a gentleman of high breeding, he had immediately commanded her attention. His soft brown eyes, his lips encircled by a mustache and short, well-trimmed beard gave his whole face a pleasing and attentive expression. Above all, his voice was always modulated and subdued, so opposite of Lord Henry Herbert's raucous utterances. Matthew had been a listening post to all her complaints, a rock that she leaned on. He was a steady fire that warmed her both day and night.

Mary Sidney had gone to Spa, Belgium, to experience its milder weather and the recuperative powers of its baths. Now fifty-three years old, she had left England with her forty-three-year-old companion, to enjoy the natural mineral springs that were said to purge the body of diseases and cure fevers. Spa was a draw for people of means for its climate, waters, and freedom to come and go without restrictions. One day, as she strolled along the spa grounds with her newfound companions, she reflected on her life's journey. She turned to her close confidant, the Countess Barlemont of Luxembourg, and described her feelings.

"My daughter is gone, and my sons are busy acting like sycophants at court. Now I may do as I please, Maria, and what pleases me is to write verse and enjoy pleasures that have been forbidden to me."

"Yes, Mary. You have done your duty to your husband, your children, your king, and God, as I have. Let us smoke, shoot pistols, dance, hunt, and play as we wish."

"I feel giddy at the thought of such freedom." She felt like a prisoner released from his chains and running wild, wanting to gulp the air, taste the wine and all the earthly delights that were formerly forbidden to him.

Emboldened by the distance from England and King James and her sons, Mary decided to break another law, namely, to marry a commoner, her lover Matthew Lister. It had been fourteen years since she had met and fallen in love with Matthew Lister. Their attraction to each other had been immediate. He was a man of science; she, a lover of and dabbler in chemistry. He was of a quiet nature, reserved and thoughtful, as well as considerate and respectful of women; she was of a more fiery temperament, impatient with inefficiency and intolerant of idleness. Their lives became forever entwined when he helped her solve the problem of her daughter's future life. For his assistance in that mission, she would be forever grateful. They both desired to wed, even if their sacred vows to each other were never made public. For Mary, marrying again meant losing her inheritance if it was ever discovered; her late husband's will stipulated as much. If found out, she would also incur the king's wrath for marrying a doctor who was considered beneath her, and her act would be subject to punishment. At least, she was well beyond child-bearing and could not taint the noble lines with half-blood children. And she wanted to have the last laugh on the king who had prevented her daughter from marrying a handsome young nobleman. He could not stop this marriage.

So far, Mary had basked in the warmth of her good luck in keeping her activities secret: her daughter's death, her sonnets and plays that either were published anonymously or were unauthorized works by William Shakespeare, the actor. This next secret was fraught with danger, which, by now, was second nature to her.

On a Sunday in late 1614, she and Matthew wed in a small church in a town not far from Spa, with her close friend Countess Maria Margaret and a few others in attendance, all sworn to keep this marriage secret to their grave. The irony of it was not lost on her. She had been duty bound to marry Henry Herbert, three times her age, and by obeying the conventions of the Crown, she had gone to Wilton House and eventually met Dr. Lister there. She had been bound by her husband's will never to marry again or she would lose her fortune, and here she was, doing the very thing forbidden to her.

"How strange it is to be marrying again, this time to a man of my own choosing. It seems the times are finally in my favor."

But only if their secret marriage did not get out. Already there were whispers of her unnaturally close friendship with Matthew. She had to return to England and to Court for events at some time, and then, if her secret became known, she would be disgraced and impoverished. She had been clever keeping her other secrets, and she felt certain that this one was worth the risk. She was marrying the man of her choice for her own personal happiness. It made her a rightful wife before God and gave her the satisfaction of having taken to her bosom a soulmate. She was no longer possessed by a man but an equal to him, loved and appreciated for her abilities, wit, and competence as well as for her beauty. Her joy was immense. She wrote to a friend from her residence in Spa, "For if you saw me now, you would say it had created a new creature."

Her family knew nothing, of course. William had still not been made Lord Chamberlain, but there were rumors that he was about to receive that powerful position. If William received that title, he would have the power to allow her plays to be published anonymously. All of her wishes would be fulfilled.

Mary and William had not spoken in ten years, but Mary continued to send him plays she had written, expecting that he would pass them on to The Lord Chamberlain's Men or some other acting company.

Her son Philip was a regular at court after King James came to the throne, and had married the daughter of an earl and was made Earl of Montgomery after which he received lands which earned him a comfortable income. As his crowning achievement, he was made Knight of the Garter, a position of the highest order.

Both her sons had managed to please the king whose debauchery and misogyny were well known. She gritted her teeth every time she thought of what they must have done to gain standing at Court. The legacy of the Sidney name, a name that she kept and valued because of its rich heritage, at one time so respected and valued, was being blotted out. Not even her learned daughter Anne was around to clean up the family history of the grime and grossness that now clung to its pages. Had she done the right thing with Anne? Did Anne's life at Wilton have merit? Did Anne's stubbornness to live and die on her own terms make her sacrifice worth it? Mary prayed that it had.

Chapter Four

Winter 1615–1616

Spa, Belgium

To Be Old and Merry

"Ready, aim, fire!" A crack was heard and a gasp went up from the crowd as Lady Mary Sidney shot a pistol whose bullet hit quite close to the middle of her target. A group of aristocrats from England and on the Continent were taking in the pleasures of the rich on the grounds of a resort in Spa, Belgium.

"Who was that meant for, Lady Mary?" said an onlooker.

"Perhaps for one who writes doggerel and calls it poetry," she replied. Her audience chuckled. She put the pistol down and took another puff from her cigarette, thoroughly enjoying pastimes that would have been scandalous during her years at Wilton House. All through the long English winters, family and friends came to Spa, bringing gossip from the court, letters from her family and friends, as well as newly printed books from the English publishers that quieted her insatiable thirst for learning. At age fifty-five, she was still lusty, still merry, still witty, and still formidable.

"The next shot is for Edmund Matthew who stole my jewels and was never punished. He will get his yet, if not in this world, then in the next."

This time her bullet hit the dead center of the target, and the gathering went wild.

Sir Henry Carew, an old friend of Mary's, called to her from across the garden.

"If I ever did you wrong, my lady, let me repent now for I would not like to be a target of your hostility."

"You, my friend, are a target of my hospitality. You have nothing to repent but rather are in very good repute."

"It is a relief to hear that I have not overstayed my visit at your lodgings, but you make me feel so welcome. I do not wish to quit this comfortable life. Some call us the idle rich, but that slur is made by people who would do the same if only they had the means."

"Sir Henry, I, for one, am never idle. If I am not shooting, I am reading or writing or at cards. I know the doctors here discourage mental activities, but I believe that the mind must be kept in constant motion. Tis the sane mind as well as the sound body that keeps us fit. Let our minds wither, and we shall be as batty as hens."

"I have heard, Lady Mary, that you write as much in a month as what other authors produce in a lifetime. And on so many different subjects," Carew responded.

"I can tell you that is true," Dr. Lister broke in, knowing that Mary did not want to be quizzed about her secret writings and switching the discussion to science. "And in her laboratory, Lady Mary concocts recipes for many illnesses and curses like seasickness, women's complaints, and other common ailments. She and Adrian Gilbert experiment with alchemy, chemistry, and other matters. There is no subject that is left unexplored."

"Yes. She even creates memory games to entertain us," said Countess Maria. "Mary, how do you manage to remember long strings of numbers forwards and backwards after days or weeks have passed by? Tell us your trick, or we shall be forced to conclude that you are a sorceress."

"They are simple pleasures to while away the time and keep boredom at bay," Mary shrugged. She looked around at the gathering who appeared to be in awe of what she considered effortless creations of her creative mind. *How I would love to tell them my secrets,* she thought. *How, after Philip's death, I swore to write the sonnets and plays that he never lived to compose. How every waking moment I thought about the stories that Philip brought back from his journey throughout the Continent, and the chronicles depicting English history that lined the shelves of my childhood home, and the stirring Greek and Roman poetry taught to me by my tutor. How I wished to take all that knowledge and beauty and transform it into English poetry and prose.*

She had been thinking back to how it all began, but lately she was more concerned with how it would all end.

Chapter Five

Winter 1615–1616
London
Power and the Purse

Late in 1615 King James I finally appointed William Herbert as Lord Chamberlain. When William arrived at court at midday to receive his charge, he found the king wrapped in a dressing gown, watching a courtier dance to the tune of a fiddler while he himself nibbled on fruits and nuts. An empty wine glass was being refilled, while two of his favorites, George Villiers and William's brother Philip, were enjoying a clown's repartee about certain notables. William nodded to his brother who, like himself, was trying to please the king by whatever means in order to secure more titles.

"I know you have wanted this post for a long time, Sir William. With your new powers, I expect you to have strict control on what is allowed to be published."

"Yes, Your Highness. I will keep the printers under my thumb. They will be granted licenses only as you command."

"I have been told there are printers who are inserting the names of popular bards on anonymous works in order to increase the sales. You must put a stop to that practice."

"Of course, Your Highness."

"Printing presses are sprouting up everywhere. It could be very dangerous to allow them to print whatever they like. I demand that every published work must first have a license."

"Yes, Your Highness. I will permit only legitimate verse to be printed and then only by their true authors, although that dictate may prove hard to enforce. As soon as one printer is found out, another magically appears. The desire for profit overrules the regard for the law."

"You have my spies at your disposal. Use them to ferret out pamphlets and treatises that are dangerous to the Crown."

William had finally achieved his lifelong objective, to be the second most powerful man in England. His mother was in Belgium where she heard that her son had become Lord Chamberlain in England. Mary remained on the Continent, traveling with Matthew to France, the Netherlands, and back to Belgium.

"I am happy for him, of course, but I am elated for a very selfish reason: What I have yearned for is now within my grasp. He cannot stop me if I tell him that I will publish my plays without his permission."

Matthew listened and shook his head.

"But you have not spoken to him for many years. Now that he has such power, he may not want to use it generously."

"Then I must return to England and go to visit him and win him over. I will play the part of a humble woman, not of a mother who has been betrayed. I am determined to have my plays published together before I die."

Mary and Matthew returned to England later that year, but the mother and son reunion did not go well.

"Good day, Mother," was all he said, but it was how he said it that gave Mary dread. William's matter-of-fact tone, along with the smirk on his face, exuded great satisfaction at having proved her wrong about his past behavior being a liability to him.

Mary stood across from William and his wife in the great hall at Wilton House where he and his wife now lived, his inheritance for being the eldest son. Although the air was perfumed with newly cut flowers, the tension between mother and son was nevertheless perceptible as was the tension between William and his wife. He had married Mary Talbot, a short, plump woman with nothing much to admire except her family wealth. William was still a tall, handsome, well-figured man, although his cheeks were red from too much tippling and his girth had broadened from too much indulging. The couple stood stiffly, separated by a few feet from each other in distance but by miles in affection. William had once again taken up with his old mistress, Mary Fitton, who after being impregnated by him years ago, continued their love affair. The smile painted on Mary Talbot Herbert's lips was artificial, but the pain reflected in her eyes was real. It was a marriage predicated on wealth and status only. At thirty-five years of age, Lord and Lady Herbert, childless and cheerless, had to live with each other until death.

Mary moved forward and kissed her daughter-in-law on both cheeks, a custom she carried back from the Continent. Then she turned to greet William.

"I pray you both are enjoying peace and a quiet life that living here inspires. This house has many memories for me, some painful but most joyous." Mary looked at William for affirmation, but he looked away. He was in no mood to give veracity to her words. His wife nodded, unsmiling, and looked sickened by having to pretend to have feelings for her indifferent husband. Mary stared with pity at the mismatched couple. *This is a poor way to begin a visit in which I must ask for William's help,* she thought.

They left the great hall to view the extravagant changes William had made to the house. More ornate columns and gilded cornices had replaced simpler ones; impressive art from the masters on the Continent crammed every first floor room. His income, which had substantially increased after he was named Lord Chamberlain, allowed him to indulge in making Wilton House one of England's finest manors.

Mary took it all in, giving William the praise and satisfaction that he was looking for. Eventually they came to an elegant sitting room where they were served costly wine and dessert. William's wife excused herself to attend to a household matter. Finally mother and son were left alone. Mary finally worked her way into bringing up the matter of her plays.

"I am vexed by seeing my plays performed and enjoyed by so many, only to be lost and forgotten if not set to print in a proper fashion. You have the power to see them published and that is what I beg you to do. Allow them to be printed all together as the work of one author."

"Mother, it is an outrageous expense to have all of your plays published in one book. I will not allow them to be licensed."

"Please, William, I beg of you. Do not have these plays vanish like the flame of a spent candle. You dishonor my brother Philip. You dishonor the muses of poetry and literature. I will pay for the cost, even though it will sorely diminish the heft of my purse."

William was not swayed, and Mary left Wilton House defeated yet again. *He would not accede to my wishes, at least not yet. He was still new to his great office; I would make another attempt later on.* If all else failed, Mary decided to find a printer on her own. Then what could her son do? Imprison his mother for publishing plays that theatergoers, rich and poor, noble and common clamored to see? She knew he would never bring such shame on his family.

Chapter Six

April 1616
Stratford-on-Avon, England
The Man Shakespeare

On April 25, 1616, William Shakespeare was buried without fanfare in the graveyard of Holy Trinity Church in his hometown. He was fifty-nine years old and had been away from London for several years.

No one is sure about the actual date of his death, only the date of his burial. He was presumed to have died on April 23rd, two days before his interment.

No one is sure about the cause of his death, only that he had drunk heavily on the night of April 22nd.

He left nothing of literary value. No books, no plays, no poems, not one single item that connected him to the trove of works that would eventually be accredited to him.

During his lifetime, he was known mainly as an actor and part owner of the Globe Theater. In the early 1590s he was accused of stealing the works of poets and publishing them with his name listed as editor on the front cover.

It was the custom for poets to write a eulogy upon the death of a fellow poet, such as occurred upon the deaths of Christopher Marlowe,

Thomas Kyd, and Philip Sidney. No eulogies were penned about William Shakespeare when he died and he never wrote a eulogy about anyone, not on the tragic death of Marlowe and not even for Elizabeth I, an ardent theatergoer and admirer of "Shakespeare's plays," upon her death in 1603.

It was only years later, when folios of the plays attributed to him were published, that poets accepted his authorship and wrote tributes honoring William Shakespeare.

Chapter Seven

1616–1619
London

Tomorrow and Tomorrow and Tomorrow

As for Lady Mary, the Countess of Pembroke created a new life for herself and Matthew. The following year she had a home built near the town of Ampthill in Bedfordshire. She called it Houghton House. It was an elegant mansion with commanding views of the English countryside, and she and Matthew entertained family and friends there for several years.

She still needed to write. It was as natural to her as breathing. She had begun a ritual after Anne had gone of putting her thoughts to paper as soon as she woke. Every morning she rose and went almost immediately to her study. There, comfortably surrounded by the ever increasing multitude of books on every subject that men could imagine, she picked up a quill pen and fashioned together words that never before stood side by side on a page. When she did not find an existing word that fit into her verse, she created one, cobbled together from other, simpler utterances. Words like green-eyed, star-crossed, ever-fixed, still-gazing, lily-livered, in fact, several thousand new word combinations that came to her as naturally as a moth to a flame.

Mary looked around her and used the images she saw in one setting and gave them new life in another. From her pastime with sewing and embroidery, she wrote of how "Sleep knits up the raveled sleave of care," and "I'll knit it up in silk strings…" Many of the common household images that women see in their lives every day were put down in her verses. She described childbirth ("the pleasing punishment that women bear"), breastfeeding ("I have given suck, and know how tender 'tis to love the babe that milks me"), and the pain of a child's ingratitude ("How sharper than a serpent's tooth to have a thankless child").

She described kneading, baking, stewing, and basting to create visual scenes in the reader's eye. "Ay, to the leavening…, the kneading, the making of the cake, the heating of the oven and the baking …"

Her interest in lawn bowling, a sport reserved for the nobility, inspired her to write images using bowl, throw, bias, and rub, all terms familiar to that sport.

As for descriptions of fights and battles, which she deplored after her brother died during a war with Spain, she used the most cursory terms to describe armed conflict: "They fight" or "As two spent swimmers, that do cling together and choke their art." She described in greater depth the psychological toll of taking up arms rather than the glory of war.

Mary's writing, as with every author's writing, reflected the life around her, the life she lived. Each sonnet was an expression of an emotion, a joy, a love, a sorrow, or a grief that begged to be made eloquent. Each play was a piece of her past, whether it was a history of her beloved England that made the audiences proud, or a tragedy of a deep loss that made the audiences weep, or a comedy full of wit and wisdom that made the audiences chuckle. Even though, with Shakespeare now dead, she could never publish these works under his name, she kept on writing. As long as she had ink and a goose pen, she continued to spin her tales and weave her plots using her powers of observation to enliven her imagination.

Mary Sidney

William Shakespeare

William Herbert

Dr. Matthew Lister

BOOK FOUR

Sarah Burton and Mary Sidney

Chapter One

February 1619
Southampton, England
Discovered

As the years dragged on, Sarah continued her passion: growing herbs and medicinal plants, devouring every book she could find on science, especially Sir Francis Bacon's work on the advancement of learning. She yearned to examine the insides of dead bodies, to understand what caused plagues, and to prevent plagues and pestilences from ever happening again. But she was without the knowledge or advice of those who had scientific training. Her father was dead, and her husband had no background in medicine. She had no one to assist her, to advise her, or to lead her to those who had greater knowledge.

At age forty-one, she felt more unfulfilled in Southampton than she had ever felt at the Mews. Going through the motions of waking, dressing, cooking, and caring for others filled her days, but she hungered for more. There was no sense of regret in what she had done to end up there, just deep dissatisfaction that her curiosity and energies were not being directed in a more satisfying way.

Robert tried to lose himself in his work as well. Some days he felt like a monk in an abbey, hidden from contact with most of humanity. All there was left to do after leaving the shipping office was return home to sit and stare out to sea. The deep love that he felt for Sarah never wavered; it was the change of his rank in the world that ate at him. He grew tired of his repetitive task, day after day, week after week, year after year. He was jealous that Sarah had much variety in her daily routine, while he had none. He had envisioned his life to be much different, even after marrying Sarah. Was he to die at his desk without leaving any mark in the world that he had passed through, without having done something of note? It seemed so.

One rainy evening Robert stayed extra late at a tavern in Southampton, drinking with the sailors and tradesmen who spent their hard-earned wages on rum and beer.

"Robert, when are you going back to France? It must have been hard to leave those beautiful mam'selles?"

"I miss the tasty dishes more than the ladies."

"Well, I hear there are tasty dishes among the ladies, Dudley."

A roar of laughter went up, which drew the attention of a spy for King James. He came over to where Robert was sitting and eyed him curiously. Robert paid him no regard, totally disarmed by the drink and the merriment around him.

"I knew a Robert Dudley, who was an earl. Any relation?"

Without thinking, Robert replied, "Ah, yes, he was a cousin and something of a scoundrel."

"Well, then, I am arresting you in the name of King James for you are quite a scoundrel yourself."

Robert looked at the man through bleary eyes, the words barely penetrating his muddled brain.

"What-what did you say?"

"You are wanted by the Crown for marrying a commoner. Thought you'd gotten away with it, did ye?"

For the first time Robert became aware of what danger he and his family were in. Through clouded thoughts he realized he was headed to trial and probably prison. As he was being led out of the ale house, he frantically looked around him, searching for someone he could trust. He spied a fellow clerk and shouted to him, "Let my wife know what has happened."

The man nodded, and Robert was taken to the local jail where he would spend the night.

When Robert did not return home that evening, Sarah began to wonder if he had been involved in a bar room brawl. The next day Robert's friend sent word to Sarah that her husband had been arrested and was being taken to London to stand trial. She had feared this event, even prepared for it, and now that it was here, she felt a strange sense of relief. Their days of running and hiding out were over. Whatever Robert's punishment would be, was up to the king. She knew what she must do to survive until he was returned to her.

Lizzie, now age twelve, had known nothing of this. Robert and Sarah did not deem it necessary to relate to her the history of their relationship until circumstances made it impossible to conceal it further. The explanation of where Robert had gone was left to Sarah. Sarah did her best to limit the details to the bare essentials. However, Lizzie was a bright student, having been tutored by both parents in a curriculum as expansive as their own.

After breakfast, when the bread and butter, along with watered down beer had been consumed, Lizzie's persistent questions about her father's absence had to be addressed. Sarah sat Lizzie down in the parlor by the windows that overlooked the confluence of the two rivers, defining

Southampton's southern border. It was her favorite spot to read, to sew, and to teach Lizzie all of the subjects that her father had taught her. Now she was forced to instruct her in the ways of the Court. Sarah began with the words she dreaded to say out loud.

"Your father has disobeyed the king and is in prison."

"Did he do a bad thing?"

"Yes. He married me."

"Why was that bad?"

"Because, Lizzie, my dear, your father is of noble birth and he is bound by the dictates of the king. A person of noble birth must only marry another noble person and I am a commoner."

"But why is it so bad to marry a commoner?"

"Because noble blood is believed to be purer than the blood of a commoner and therefore can only be kept pure through noble marriages."

"I don't understand how it is purer. Is it because they are richer than everyone else?"

"No. Being rich doesn't change a person's blood."

"Are they smarter?"

"Not necessarily. They, as a whole, are better educated because they have books and tutors readily available to them."

"Well, are they more holy?"

Sarah frowned as she remembered rumors about King James delighting in illicit acts with both men and women as well as the cruelty shown by royalty over the last several centuries.

"No. Their blood is purer because they say it is purer."

"Well, I say let them prove it! I am glad Papa married you."

Sarah smiled and said, "Your father gave up a life of ease and influence to marry me. He is no longer a nobleman; instead he is a man of noble spirit, which is much better. I am very fortunate to have your father as my husband."

While she awaited word on his fate, Sarah offered her services as a midwife and a healer to all comers. Expectant mothers knew they could depend on her to ease their pain and facilitate a birth no matter what the hour. Her knowledge of plants and cures for common ailments was in much demand among the sailors, dock workers, and laborers who always seemed to have injuries and sicknesses. Besides earning an income and feeling useful, Sarah was grateful for the distraction from the terrible thoughts of Robert in jail. The man who had sacrificed his future, his inheritance for her and who fathered her miracle child had been taken away from her by the dictates of the Crown.

The king had sentenced Robert to two years of incarceration in the Tower of London. His crime: marrying a commoner without royal permission. Sarah wanted to go to London to be near him but had no way to survive there. In Southampton, she was called upon as a midwife, an herbalist, and a dispenser of medical knowledge and treatments. She would never be allowed to go to medical school to be a doctor, but she had found a calling that was important and honorable. Here she was known and trusted; London was impossibly far and purportedly dangerous. There were days when she ministered to sick children and expectant mothers from first light to pitch blackness. Her energy and resilience grew with each life she saved and with each child she delivered. Sometimes she felt her father's presence as she tended fevers and treated wounds.

When, in the dark hours of the night, she tossed and turned wondering how all these things turned out so badly and second-guessing the choices she had made, the thought of the king's absolute power over everyone in the kingdom drove her to wish for an escape. She did not want to live in England any more. As soon as she and Robert were reunited, she was going to ask him if they could leave their tortured life there and sail to the New World, where there were no spies, no Tower of London, no family history. The more she thought about it, the more excited she became. A new beginning for them both.

Chapter Two

Spring 1620
The Mews
A Glimpse of the Past

Years after burying her father beside her mother in the family grave at the Mews, Sarah took Lizzie back into her childhood home for one last time. She needed money, and the Mews was the only asset she had left to sell. It had sat empty for years, and the neglect by its owner was evident everywhere she looked. A leaky roof, a broken window, a chewed page from a book. How sad her father would be to see his family home in such a dilapidated state. She walked around the rooms, committing to memory objects that were dear to her, the portrait of her grandfather, the oak chair by the fire, the medical bag, worn and battered from constant use. In the library, she walked past rows of shelves crammed with books and manuscripts on every subject from many countries in various tongues. These were her father's most precious possessions. When she touched them, she felt her father's presence, his soft voice, his warm smile, his gentle touch. With a heavy heart, she gathered up a few books that she could sell immediately while she waited for a prospective buyer to make an offer. She was making her way out of the library when something red caught her eye on a bottom shelf. It was a red ribbon wrapped around a package which was half hidden behind a book. She read the lettering on the front: For Sarah.

She sat in her father's chair by the fireside and began to untie the ribbon that bound it together. As she unwrapped the frayed bundle of papers, a small black box fell to the floor. Tentatively, she picked it up and looked at it, questioningly. She stared at the box and wondered what was inside. She and her father had no secrets from each other; each had understood the other's nature and felt comfortable in their father-daughter relationship. She decided to examine the papers first. They contained correspondence from his wide circle of friends, personal letters from notables he had met in his travels and a letter from her mother to her father dated the year of their marriage. It was a loving note, telling him how much she missed him and that the preparations for their marriage were complete. Sarah reread it several times and clutched it to her chest. It was the most personal thing she had of a mother she never knew.

On her lap rested the black box, large enough to hold an egg. She carefully lifted the lid and looked down at its contents. Staring back at her was a lady's gold ring with a large square-cut emerald in its center and her father's signet ring with the letter B etched on a black enamel stone. Sarah lifted the lady's ring and looked on the inside for an engraved message. She read the words aloud. "To Mary Love John." She started to sob. "This was my mother's ring. Why did my father not show it to me?" Then she remembered that whenever she asked questions about her mother, her father would turn away and say simply, "Not now." Perhaps his grief at her sudden death prevented him from ever looking at it again. She slipped it on her ring finger which had always been bare, for she had convinced Robert that spending precious money on a piece of jewelry was an extravagance that they could not afford. It fit perfectly, and she swore she would never remove it. It was a link to her past, to a beloved wife and to the woman who gave her life. She would also keep her father's ring, it being a precious reminder of his love and his selflessness in assenting to let her live apart from him for the rest of her life. Now that she had a child of her own, she understood what a sacrifice that must have been.

Despite her desperate need of money, she felt that selling her family home, a property that went back generations to when her great-grandfather built it in the early 1500s, would be a betrayal to her ancestors. Each succeeding generation had enlarged and remodeled it so that it became the finest home in the area. She took more of the books that still filled the library shelves to sell but made a silent promise to her father that she would keep the property for as long as possible.

Chapter Three

Summer 1620
London
Free at Last

One day in early July, 1620, two females, newly arrived, walked through the streets of London, each with a travel bag in hand, and cast their eyes about, searching for a street whose name was written on a scrap of paper. The couple, mother and daughter, were dressed in their best holland linen garments which, despite the heat, had to cover everything but their face and hands for propriety's sake. They appeared to be respectable commoners, not rich enough to afford silks and satins, but not so poor as to be clad in buckram. Sarah Burton had kept in touch with Robert's sister through the use of musical codes that Mary Sidney had provided her. Elizabeth was now living in London with her husband and children. Sarah prayed that they had not left the city to escape the heat and pestilence that often accompanied it. She so much wanted to see her sister-in-law again and to understand why no one of influence could free Robert. It was not hard to discover the home of Lord and Lady Davies, a prominent manor in one of the nicest areas of the city.

"Elizabeth, it is you. You are much changed but yet are much the same." Sarah noticed that Elizabeth's girth had widened and furrows lined her brow, but her bright eyes and curly brown hair still made her a most attractive woman.

"I can say the same for you. I am delighted to see you and tell you that I have visited Robert several times and he is in good spirits, considering all that has happened. When you see him, you will confirm that. I have made several attempts, through my husband, of course, to have Robert freed, but King James takes his time on these matters. It is nothing to him to have a nobleman imprisoned while his royal majesty enjoys the luxuries of the court. But the king has agreed to Lord Davies' request that you be allowed to visit him."

"Please tell your husband that I am most grateful for his intervention."

"Of course. He is an amiable man and attentive to my wishes. The fact that he is ten years older has made no difference in our respect for each other. I feel quite lucky, in fact." Her surroundings confirmed that Elizabeth had married a wealthy man. Her manor, a building erected in the 1500s, was a three-story affair, tastefully decorated with silk curtains on the windows and Doric columns between walls covered with floral wallpaper. Elizabeth led Sarah and Lizzie to a sitting room with high-backed mahogany chairs and inlaid tables, her favorite room for entertaining guests.

"Elizabeth, I am so happy for you. Your present condition is what you had hoped for during our shopping trip so many years ago. I have no such wants. I just miss Robert dearly. If it wasn't for Lizzie who keeps me comforted, I would surely be heartsick."

"He worries most about how you and Lizzie are getting along and what he will do when he is released. His past will always follow him wherever he goes in England."

"Yes, I have been concerned about that as well." She was tempted to tell Elizabeth of her desire to sail to the colonies, but thought better of it. She had not yet discussed it with Robert. "We will make do. I am sure of it."

"Of course, you will. You both have such strong spirits and your feminine wiles have provided you with an income during these hard times. Do you know that Lady Mary Sidney is presently in London ? You should go to see her at the house where she lives for she asks about you when I visit her. It is not far from here." And so Sarah found herself sitting across from Mary in a sitting room at her imposing residence on Aldgate Street, pouring her heart out to a woman she had met only once before. She told how she and Robert had been discovered in Rouen and fled to Southampton soon after her daughter was born, how Robert obtained work as a scrivener at a merchant's establishment on the waterfront. She told how her daughter had almost died from the plague and how, miraculously, she had recovered on a visit to her father whom she had so dearly wanted to see again but hadn't because she feared for his safety, how Robert's incarceration was due to his being so distraught at his life in perpetual hiding that he became careless for his own welfare, but now, in letters to her, deeply regretted his imprudent behavior at the tavern. Sarah had come to London, with her daughter, having no connections to the Crown, to see Robert and try to have him released from the Tower. He was a kindred spirit who understood her moods and allowed her the freedom to do and say what she pleased. When Sarah was out of breath, she hung her head, not daring to see the countess's reaction. Her eyes were wet from weeping and she thought of how Lady Mary had bravely suffered her own hardships, including her daughter's death and how weak she herself must appear in comparison.

Mary sat silent for a long time, staring out the window. Finally she asked the servant who was standing by the door to leave. Mary bent toward Sarah and whispered, "Perhaps we can help each other."

Within a month, Robert was released from prison, by order of the king and at the urging of William Herbert, the Lord Chamberlain. It was Mary's doing, of course. She had implored her son to have Robert released after he had served only half his sentence. William had petitioned the king and his Highness had grudgingly agreed. Robert Dudley was William's cousin, and William knew what being imprisoned in the Tower was like, having been sent there by Queen Elizabeth I for impregnating her lady-in-waiting, Mary Fitton.

What Mary wanted in exchange for her cousin Robert's release was simple. As a scrivener, he was capable of making fair copies, error-free copies, of the plays she had written and so prepare them for the printer. It was an enormous task. Thirty-seven plays to be exact. Robert's handwriting would not be recognized and Mary's secret kept hidden. Even though William Shakespeare's name would be listed as author, there was the danger that some skeptic might find that hard to believe and look for the original manuscripts. Robert was grateful to have work. It meant that he had employment in London and his cousin Mary could publish her works in secret. Such a satisfactory solution to their problems seemed to be heaven-sent.

Chapter Four

August 1621

London

The Plays' the Thing

"I can smell the pox."

Even before Mary had exited from her coach, she sensed the danger. She sniffed the air and licked her lips as though it was a tangible thing floating past her. Like an unwanted visitor, smallpox dropped in without warning, made itself comfortable, and refused to leave until it had spent its presence making everyone else miserable.

In spite of the danger, Mary came to London anyway, many months later than she had originally thought. Her travel plans had been disrupted by a royal request. King James, wishing to leave the hot and disease-filled city of London during the summer, sent a missive to the Countess, desiring to visit Houghton House in mid-July. That meant that there would be hundreds of people in his retinue whom she was expected to feed, entertain, and bed. This one visit alone would cost Mary thousands and thousands of pounds, money that she had planned to use for another enormous expense, but she could not refuse a king's "request." On July 21st, King James came north with his servants, bodyguards, ministers, and courtesans. She did everything she could to shoo him and his minions out as quickly as possible.

By mid-August she was prepared to carry out her scheme. The plays—her plays—were going to be handed over to the printers as anonymous works. She sensed that her life was nearly at its end and it was time to act, on her own, without getting the necessary license from her son, the Lord Chamberlain.

As for the pox, perhaps she thought she was immune to the contagion because in infancy, she had been exposed to it firsthand. It had ravaged her mother's face when, while helping Queen Elizabeth recover from the disease, Lady Mary Dudley Sidney had contracted it. She survived, but was marred for life, with horrible looking pits on her face. For ever after, she wore a veil in public to hide her disfigurement. Her baby daughter Mary had escaped untouched.

Now fifty-eight years later, Mary was tempting fate by going into the heart of London during the pox's breeding season while others were fleeing from it. She had more pressing matters at hand: to see the culmination of over forty years of writing works that elevated the English language and would endure forever. Her son William had refused her request to allow them to be published anonymously many times before, but hopefully, he had mellowed. She decided to approach him on the matter one last time. He not only refused her request, he railed at its lunacy. The cost would be prohibitive. She might be found out. His titles and offices would be taken away. He would be disgraced. She must be senile to even entertain the thought.

Mary left his residence in London in a foul mood, angry at his reaction, though by now, not really surprised. Time was running out. She had to act on her own. As long as her name wasn't listed as the author, there was no way that the printed plays could be connected to her, and both her sons' reputations would be protected. The cost to publish thirty-seven plays would be very costly, but at this final stage in her life, what need did she have for money? The aches and pains associated with aging told her that more travel to the Continent was not advisable. She was now in the final act of her life, the scene where the conflict that existed during most of her time on Earth was resolved.

It was important that she find a scrivener to make fair copies, and there was only one person that she could trust. Robert Dudley, her distant cousin, a newly released prisoner and a practiced scrivener, suited her needs perfectly. He came to her Aldgate Street home and labored over them for ten hours each day. In August of 1621 Mary Sidney and Dr. Matthew Lister went to the establishment of Edward Blount and William and Isaac Jaggard. The doctor carried a sizable purse and fair copies of five unlicensed plays, promising that he would return in a few months with additional plays. The printers had been reluctant, not wishing to disobey the Crown, but the size of the purse on their desk convinced them it was worth the risk. The printing started immediately.

Lady Mary had gambled that the pox wanted nothing to do with her, but in the late summer of 1621, her luck ran out. The pestilence sprung out from its hiding place in the filthy trenches of fetid lanes and landed on her doorstep, with full force. She woke up one morning in early September feeling feverish and tired. Within a day a rash appeared over most of her body, accompanied by a severe headache. She had seen enough of its scourge and of its voracious appetite to know how things would end. She wrote her will, revealing her marriage to Matthew Lister and leaving her lover/husband a generous annual allowance as well as the disposition of all her writings.

She was not afraid to die. Her faith in God had always sustained her through the deaths of many loved ones and through the shame and humiliation brought on by her sons, William in particular.

"I go to my Creator willingly, thankful for the long and full life He has granted me and I repent of my sins. My Lord has given me the greatest comfort in my life—you, dear Matthew. You have borne my infirmities without complaint. You have been my most faithful friend. You are my true and honorable husband."

Matthew tried in every way to comfort her, but there was no let-up in its progression. Within a few weeks, it had weakened her body beyond recovery. On September twenty-first, a month before her sixtieth birthday, Lady Mary Sidney Herbert, the Countess of Pembroke, died at her London home, with Matthew Lister at her bedside.

Her funeral was one of the biggest ever held in London at the time. Over one hundred coaches lined the street to St. Paul's Cathedral, and then the torchlight funeral procession continued all the way to the magnificent Salisbury Cathedral where she was buried alongside her first husband, Lord Henry Herbert. Tributes came from men and women of literature, including the feminist poet Emilia Lanier who penned "she was esteemed for virtue, wisdom, learning and dignity" and "She will be the eyes, the hearts, the tongues, the ears of after-coming ages." John Donne called her "Miriam" or beloved; a tribute by poet William Browne spoke of Mary as "the subject of all verse" and "fair and learned." Her secretary John Davies declared that if Mary thirsted for fame as men do, she would let it "come to light." Gabriel Harvey described Mary as "the gentlest, and wittiest, and bravest, and invincibliest gentlewoman that I know."

Her good friend Ben Jonson referred to her as gentle and having a silvered tongue. His eulogy to the author of the First Folios sounded like an ode to a woman, not a man. He described the writer of the plays as a "sweet swan of Avon" and that the poet of these works should become a muse when, curiously, all the other muses were women. Matthew Lister received a substantial income each year from her estate even though Mary's will was said to have never been found.

Many of her writings disappeared.

A few weeks later, in October, the printing of the plays suddenly stopped. Months later the printing began again with Ben Jonson as editor. The first folio, finally published in 1623 and printed on paper that was better than what was used for most Bibles, was dedicated to the Herbert brothers, William and Philip, and listed William Shakespeare as author.

Chapter Five

May 1629

Yarmouth, England

Seeing Is Believing

After Mary Sidney died, Robert's means of earning a living as her scrivener died as well. He had sworn not to tell anyone in her family about what he had been doing, and he kept his promise. Such an enormous secret, if revealed, could shame and strip the Herbert and Sidney families of their long-held titles and privileges. Together with Sarah and Lizzie, he left London with the memories of the Tower still fresh in his mind. For over a year he had to ingest putrid food and inhale dank air. He wanted to blot out those wretched conditions and enjoy the company of his wife and child. They went back to the Mews to live, hoping that the house and land might be able to provide them with a decent living. On the one hand, they were thankful that they had a spot of land to scrabble a living from, but, on the other hand, they regretted that the property was in such a remote location. There was no work to be found in that area for a scrivener or a tutor, so Robert did his best as a gentleman farmer. He was better with animals than with crops and garnered a reputation for caring for sick sheep, goats, and horses. Sarah was still well-known among the inhabitants, her father still fondly remembered, and she was called on to minister to them in sickness and in childbirth.

Each time when things got really tough, they took one of Dr. Burton's books to sell in Salisbury. All in all, they earned enough money to feed and clothe themselves and Lizzie but not much more.

Both Robert and Sarah spent many hours teaching Lizzie how to read and write, how to analyze and argue, and how to doctor people and animals.

"When I am grown, I am going to be a physician like my grandfather and Mum," she declared.

"Please, do not call me a doctor. That title is not permitted to a woman, and pretending to be one could have me thrown in prison."

Her parents smiled at their daughter's overweening ambition but were secretly proud that she had the confidence to imagine it.

Between 1624 and 1628, the times became more difficult. England was again at war with France, which caused a scarcity of farmhands, while heavy rains ruined crops, producing food shortages. Small pox and the plague took turns setting down for a spell, wiping out thousands of inhabitants at each appearance. Each day, each month, and each year was a constant battle to survive. At the end of 1628, Robert and Sarah were weary and longed for an opportunity to be free of the struggle and free of the past. Together they made the decision to sell the Mews for whatever they could get and leave the Burton home for good. They considered going back to London, but neither of them wanted to be so close to the king and the Tower. With scrimping and saving and some luck, they hoped to some day sail to the New World, to a land where a man's past could be kept hidden and where all things were possible. The family of three headed for Southampton where they were told that the busiest port was now in Yarmouth, farther south.

The money they received from the sale of the house and land gave them the ability to rent an apartment by the docks in this small port city. It had become a departure point for sailing west and was teeming with activity, good for the occupations of scriveners, like Robert, and herbalists, like Sarah. While Robert labored indoors with pen and paper, trying to earn enough pence to put aside for the voyage, Sarah spent her mornings at the docks, selling her homemade remedies to sailors suffering from diseases, like dysentery and scurvy, that they contracted on board ship, or potions to help the pilgrims manage the nausea induced by the motion of the ship. She became captivated with watching Puritans sail for the New World, trying to imagine what the lands across the sea were like. She had read books describing exotic Arabian markets and magnificent Chinese temples, but no one had written much about the lands to the west. The bits and pieces of information she had overheard from sea dogs seemed impossible to be real—red men with painted faces and feathers in their hair, fish so plentiful that they jumped above the waves like silver spray, forests so thick with trees as to form a dense wall, nearly impenetrable. She admired these Puritans who dared to cross thousands of miles of ocean on a leaky caravel. They were convinced that the chance of dying was worth the risk.

One morning in August 1629 Sarah came to the crowded wharf where a caravel was preparing to leave for its two-month voyage to the New World. It was a particularly hot day in late summer and although the sun hadn't been up very long, the crowds along the waterfront were already feeling uncomfortable. Their long dark woolen and buckram garments absorbed the heat, drawing it in like a sponge. It was not proper to remove items of clothing in public, so the sweat and stench from their bodies just added to the salty, fishy odors wafting up from the sea.

The dock was packed with longshoremen wheeling carts loaded with casks to be brought on board the ship. A sailor, bent over from the weight of his duffel bag, made his way up the gangway. A one-eyed beggar nodded to Sarah as she dropped a coin in his outstretched hand; a crusty fisherman tipped his cap to her as she walked by; a pair of urchin boys zigzagged through the crowds with a flapping fish in each of their hands, undoubtedly snatched from a fishmonger's pail. Passengers, both eager and fearful for their future, said their tearful goodbyes to their families who were too old, or too sick, or too afraid to make the journey themselves.

Sarah stood on the dock with herbs in her basket, hoping to sell a seasickness remedy to the Puritans about to board a ship. She took note of a large family who stood out from the others. There were eight children, one a babe in the arms of its mother. The older children were dressed in fine cambric linen under their broadcloth woolen capes. They all had on caps or hats over curly red hair and each had fashionable leather shoes. The older children carried sturdy looking satchels. They held hands so as not to get lost on the crowded pier or fall into the deep water. While their parents chatted with other members of their group, their offspring stood in line, waiting patiently. *What handsome and well behaved children,* Sarah thought. The husband, tall, lean, and clean shaven, wore the black cloth of a minister. He put his hand on his wife's arm in a loving, reassuring way. Sarah's eyes rested on her, looking at her in profile. An unsettling feeling came over Sarah, a sense that she had seen this woman before. As they got closer to her, Sarah heard the woman speak to her children, in a warm and gentle manner.

"You must keep together and do not fuss about the small space below the deck. Any discomfort you feel will be worth the journey."

Sarah drew near and asked the mother if she needed any herbs to settle stomachs from the motions of the ship in the high seas. The woman looked at her and smiled, "Thank you kindly for your offer, but I have my own remedy for seasickness."

Sarah was surprised since it was rare for commoners to travel on the ocean.

"Have you been on an ocean voyage before?" Sarah asked.

The woman shook her head sadly.

"No, but my mother traveled frequently to Belgium and she concocted a recipe so good that she never got sick on any voyage."

"I would like to have that recipe."

Just then the line began to move and while the woman's husband and children moved ahead, his wife stopped to answer. Sarah heard him say, "You must keep up. We will be boarding shortly."

Sarah moved closer and persisted in her request.

"Perhaps I can ask your mother for the recipe. Does she live nearby?"

"No. She last lived in London. Sadly she died from the pox eight years ago. She had many recipes to relieve common ailments, but it was the pox that killed her. No recipe for that."

Sarah stared after her, dumbstruck. Mary Sidney had died from the pox in London eight years ago. She, too, had many recipes to cure common afflictions. What a coincidence!

Sarah continued to move with them and watched as the family approached the gangway. The minister turned to his wife and said, "Anne, I will go first and lead the way."

"Oh my! Oh my!" Sarah blurted out. *It can't be Anne Herbert. She's dead. The countess told me so herself.* Then she remembered that twice, when Mary had spoken of her daughter Anne, she used the present tense and had not corrected herself. At the time, Sarah had thought it was no more than a slip of the tongue.

It is Anne. It has to be her. That is why she looks so familiar.

The family of ten reached the ship's gangway and began to ascend, joining the next wave of pioneers who would brave the high seas to reach a place where one's past mattered little. They were still within hearing distance of her when, impulsively, Sarah shouted, "Anne Herbert!"

The woman spun around, looking frightened. The man turned to stare at her as well, and then urged Anne on, impatient to leave the past behind and take their one chance to live without a king or the Church dictating what they must say and do.

Sarah hesitated, not knowing what to say. There was no time to explain the enormous impact Anne's mother had had on her life: how Mary had advised her to flee England with Robert, how Mary had shared a musical code that allowed Sarah to communicate with her father, and how Mary had facilitated the early release of her husband Robert who was once engaged to Anne.

"God be with you, Anne," was all Sarah could manage to say. She waved her hand and smiled broadly.

Anne turned to look back, still puzzled, as if trying to place this figure who knew her name. Tentatively, she raised her hand in acknowledgement. As the Puritan family reached the ship's deck, Sarah gazed at them in wonder, realizing the enormity of the secret she had accidentally discovered. She shivered in spite of the August heat. Anne's death was faked. She had not died in Cambridge after all. Here she was with a husband and large family leaving England for a voyage to a land across the ocean.

Should she tell Robert of this revelation? Was it something he should know? What good would come of it? Anne had found another to wed and raise a family with. She had made a new life for herself. To tell Robert all this would only make him look at his own life and perhaps regret his decision to marry her.

And then there was the matter of his brother, Edward. She was sure that he was the one who visited her home in 1593, who asked to see her father, and who followed her into the house and attacked her so violently. He was looking for Papists but found only books, books which he determined to be evidence of a plot of some nature. Since John Burton was not home, Edward decided to punish him by attempting to have his way with his daughter. How could she ever reveal this information to Robert?

She decided that this secret, along with the other, had to remain buried in her heart forever. The following year Sarah, Robert, and Lizzie packed what little possessions they had, boarded a ship that set sail to America and the realization of their dreams.

Epilogue

Summer 1630
Plimouth, Massachusetts Bay Colony
The Hand Maid Lands in the New World

It took two long and stormy months for the caravel *Hand Maid*, carrying a cargo of hope and courage, to reach the shores of the new England. Its sixty-odd passengers consisted of mostly poor wretches who had despaired of ever improving their lot in England and now were clinging to their last chance to change their lives for the better. The rolling seas had been rough and merciless, the twenty-eight cows on board loud and smelly, and the seasick passengers green and miserable. There was nothing for the Puritans to do but cling to a railing and pray to God for an end to their present misery.

"I wished I had gotten that recipe from that woman," murmured Sarah, wistfully. She and Robert had come to the deck for some fresh air, while Lizzie slept below.

"What recipe from what woman, Sarah?" muttered Robert, clutching his stomach in despair.

Sarah hadn't realized she had spoken her thoughts loud enough for her husband to hear. "Oh, some lady who claimed her mother had concocted a recipe for seasickness that worked exceedingly well," answered Sarah, turning away to hide her discomfort at bringing up the subject.

"I wish you had, too," groaned Robert who held his stomach with one hand and a pole with the other. "Where did you meet her?"

"Oh, by the docks in Gravesend," Sarah replied, hoping Robert would stop asking questions.

"Was she selling a cure?"

"No, she and her husband and children were about to board a ship called *The Lyon's Whelp*. I asked if she needed something for seasickness and she told me that she had her mother's marvelous recipe. I hope that they made it across the ocean," she added.

"Last year that ship obtained provisions from my company and sailed for the new world. It did reach the port of Salem."

"Her husband was a minister, so his prayers probably reached God's ears faster than anyone else's."

"Perhaps you will see her again. There are not many settlements along the coast of what they are now calling new England. Plimouth and Salem are not that far from each other. If so, be sure to get the recipe. There will always be a need for it and you must include it in the recipe book you will publish. I have decided to become a printer in Boston and your book shall be my first publication. I am through with quill pens forever. "

Sarah welcomed the thought of Robert's new line of work but not the thought of the possibility of seeing Anne Herbert again, and she felt even more ill. What would happen if she accidentally met Anne Herbert along with her husband and children? Anne might recognize her and ask how Sarah knew her name. Even worse Anne and Robert might see each other again. For Robert, it would be like seeing a dead person resurrected. Sarah could not imagine such a scene.

In late October, the ship made its way into Plimouth Harbor and unloaded its passengers. The weak and weary travelers set foot on solid ground and swore that they would never travel on the ocean again. With the help of those already settled there and with good fortune, Sarah and Robert and Lizzie would survive their first winter in the New World and go on to thrive in a land where the future is bright and bountiful, and there is no longer any need to live in hugger-mugger.

Author's Note

Mary Sidney, the Countess of Pembroke (1561–1621) was a very well educated noble woman who wrote volumes and volumes of prose and poetry during her lifetime, much of which has been lost. She published poetry and translations of classical works within the parameters permitted to a person of her sex and stature at that time. Her lifespan approximated that of William Shakespeare (1564–1616), and there is much circumstantial evidence that points to her as the author of the works accredited to him.

Matthew Lister (1571–1656) became the doctor in residence at Wilton House in 1604 and remained at Mary's side until her death. There were rumors during their lifetime that he and Mary Sidney had married. In 1635, King Charles I made him a knight, which was a very unusual honor for a medical doctor to receive.

Anne Herbert (1583–1640?), Mary's daughter, was reported to have died in 1606 in Cambridge, England, after a reoccurring illness. Her tomb has never been found. Modern-day investigators have discovered that a lady named Anne Herbert was married to Francis Higginson on January 8, 1615, at St. Peter's Parish Church in Nottingham. On the church records, no parents were listed for either of them. She was mentioned as being quite literate. Francis Higginson had become a priest in the Church of England a month before. Anne and her husband Francis had eight children between 1615 and 1629. They then left England for the New World and arrived in Salem, Massachusetts, in the autumn of 1629, where Francis preached until his death just a year later. Anne took her family to Charlestown, Massachusetts, and finally moved to New Haven, Connecticut, with her son John. She died in 1640. Among her descendants are many famous Americans, including Senator George Cabot, Henry Cabot Lodge, Robert Frost, and Oliver Wendell Holmes and others.

Robert Greene was a popular author of romances and plays who wrote a pamphlet criticizing Shakespeare as well as a letter to other playwrights suggesting that there was a woman behind Shakespeare.

Sarah Burton and John Burton are fictional characters, as is young Robert Dudley. An older Robert Dudley, a suitor of Queen Elizabeth I, was the uncle of Mary Sidney.

\` \` \`

It has been nearly four hundred years since Edward Blount and William and Isaac Jaggard began to publish plays attributed to William Shakespeare. The person who paid the enormous expense for the plays to be published on the best Crown paper and thereby preserve them for posterity was very likely William Herbert, the son of Mary Sidney, Countess of Pembroke. In fact, the First Folios were dedicated to the Herbert brothers, William and Philip.

It remains a mystery as to why William Herbert, who at the time was Lord Chamberlain of England, and held the second most powerful position in the country next to the king, might have put out a considerable amount to money to see these particular plays in print. Was it because his mother, as a dying wish, had asked him to publish them altogether, listing Shakespeare as author since she could never claim them as her own?

So far there is not one document in Shakespeare's own hand that ties him to the works that bear his name. As early as 1592, he was accused of stealing plays because nobody believed that he was capable of writing such exquisite verse. Was he, in fact, needed as a beard because the real author could not publish herself, since her identity would be revealed and her family disgraced? If so, why was he chosen as the author? Perhaps he was simply a person in the right place at the right time, working as an actor and thus having legitimacy to produce copies of new plays to be performed on the stage.

If one had to list all the qualifications that the author of the "Shakespearian" plays and sonnets had to have in order to write so knowledgeably and eloquently, the one "poet" who does not measure up is William Shakespeare. But Mary Sidney does measure up, in spades. She had an education that rivaled the queen's. As a lady-in-waiting to Elizabeth I, she had first-hand knowledge of courtiers and royal etiquette. She was a countess with a noble background (sixth cousin to the queen) and who, during her lifetime, published acceptable works in accordance with her rank and sex. The death of her brother Philip, a noted poet in his day, drove her to realize his dream: to bring the English language, which languished in obscurity and coarseness, to a place of illumination and elegance.

Women writers had many restrictions placed on them: they could only pen works that did not reflect badly on their virtue, like religious translations or advice manuals for the care of children. However, during this period a few females began to discuss and publish poetry of unprecedented significance. One such poet was Emilia Lanier whose work *Salve Dues Rex Judaeorum* (1611) made the case for the equality of men and women. Another was Lady Mary Sidney whose published works *To the Angel of the Most Excellent Sir Philip Sidney* and *A Dialogue Between Two Shepherds* displayed rhyming techniques that rivaled that of Shakespeare's. (That alone makes a strong case for Mary Sidney being the "real" Shakespeare.)

Mary Sidney was a woman of secrets: she wrote in code using musical notes and invented disappearing ink. There is evidence that she helped fake her daughter Anne's death and rumors that she secretly entered into a marriage with a commoner, Dr. Matthew Lister. Those two secrets, if revealed, would have ruined her family. She, obviously, was not afraid to take chances. As her life was nearing its end, she took the biggest chance of all—to publish a complete set of her plays so they would live on in history. As luck would have it, she died just as the printing got started and it is likely that her son William took over and had them published under the name of William Shakespeare. He, too, was a lover of poetry and did not want his mother's literary accomplishments lost to future generations.

Each year more documents are discovered in libraries, manors, book shops, and other places that reveal information that what was once thought true is really false. Perhaps there is a musical score with a message encoded in its notes or a book made of fine vellum whose empty pages make its current owners think of it as having little or no value. But if a candle were to be placed close to the paper, images would emerge that will reveal lines of sonnets or plays written in hugger-mugger by Lady Mary Sidney.

Bibliography

Booth, Mark, *The Secret History of the World*, 2008, New York, NY, Overlook Press.

Faulkes, Fred, *Tiger's Heart in Woman's Hide*, vol.1, 2007, Victoria, BC, Trafford Publishing

Hannay, Margaret P., *Philip's Phoenix Mary Sidney Countess of Pembroke*, 1990, New York, NY, Oxford University Press.

Hayes, Robert, "Lady Anne Herbert: Another Wilton Secret," in the *Cignet*, Issue 2, 2013, Santa Fe, NM, Wilton Circle Press.

Mortimer, Ian, *The Time Traveler's Guide to Elizabethan England*, 2014, New York, NY, Penguin Books.

Shakespeare's Sonnets and Other Poems, 2017, San Diego, CA, Printers Row Publ. Gr.

Taylor-Davidson, Sue, *To Pluck a Crow*, Bk. 1, 2018, Canada, Renaissance Book Press.

The Arden Dictionary of Shakespeare's Quotes, Jane Armstrong, Ed., 2010, London, Methuen Publishing Ltd.

Wilkinson, Nevile Rodwell, *Wilton House Guide*, 1908, London, Chiswick Press.

Williams, Robin P., *Sweet Swan of Avon Did a Woman Really Write Shakespeare?* 2012, Santa Fe, NM, Wilton Circle Press.

Yeomans, Ann, "Soror Mystica Mary Sidney and the Alchemy of the 'Shakesperean' Canon", in the *Cignet*, Issue 3, 2017, Santa Fe, NM, Wilton Circle Press.

Young, Frances Campbell, *Mary Sidney Countess of Pembroke*, 1912, London, David Nutt.

About the author

Joyce Consolino Gatta is a retired English teacher and college professor. She earned a B.A. degree from Boston University, a M.Ed. degree from Northeastern University, and a M.Ed. degree in Special Education from Lesley University. She lives in Hudson, Massachusetts.

Credits

The cover design was suggested by her daughter Margarita Gatta.

Help and encouragement in writing this book were provided by her son Anthony Gatta and her grandson Matthew Gatta.

Jan and Dale McLean presented Joyce with a gift, a book by Robin P. Williams called *Sweet Swan of Avon Did a Woman Write Shakespeare?* which inspired this work.